Mice and Marriage

Love's Infestation Series #2

May your life be a story in faithful living

Sophie Dawson

DISCLAIMER

This is a work of fiction. Names, characters, businesses, places, events and incidents are either the products of the author's imagination or used in a fictitious manner. Any resemblance to actual persons, living or dead, or actual events is purely coincidental.

All product and company names are trademarks™ or registered® trademarks of their respective holders. Use of them does not imply any affiliation with or endorsement by them.

The LEGO company requests, on their boxes, in the fine print, and on their website, that people call their bricks LEGO rather than Legos. In the US, we tend to be rebels and use the term Legos. I don't think I've ever heard anyone refer to them as a bunch of LEGO. Somehow, I doubt the US born and raised Camden and Mark would say the floor was covered with LEGO.

DEDICATION

Over the past few years, I've been meeting regularly with a couple of friends. We support, admonish, encourage, and keep accountable to each other. We are safe to be open and vulnerable. When we don't meet, my week doesn't go as well. We lost a member to cancer recently. She will get a book dedicated to her soon. This book I dedicate to Mary. Thank you for being my friend.

ACKNOWLEDGEMENTS

As always, I want to acknowledge my team of faithful friends who help make my books as good as they are, my editor, beta readers, and advance copy readers. This time I'm not going to list the names. You know who you are. Or should. Just know that I very much appreciate your support and help. Thank you.

DESCRIPTION

Noelle Copeland has no intention of ever letting another man break her heart. She's content to take care of her two boys and help her brother around the church. That is until a mouse sends her onto a table screaming like she's being murdered, and a handsome, heroic man comes to her rescue. Now, she finds her heart longing for Turner Metcalf, but he's keeping things from her. She wonders if she can trust him not only with her heart but her sons' hearts as well.

Turner Metcalf is a man on a mission. He's in town for the Thanksgiving and Christmas season for one reason only; to protect his sister and her new husband. He has a secret life he isn't willing to give up. That is until he comes to the rescue of Noelle Copeland. Now, his heart is drawn to the one thing he never thought he could have; a future. He finds himself falling for the divorced mother of two and her sons.

Can he survive his secret mission long enough to let her know? Or will his frequent travel and hidden agenda end things before they really get started? Will he live through his mission and be able to consider a future with this ready-made family? What about Noelle's ex-husband and his new girlfriend? Will they mess things up for Noelle and Turner? Can love find a way to overcome the doubts of a woman afraid of Mice and Marriage?

Love and marriage come to us inspired by many things. Who would have thought that mold, spots and mice would bring love and marriage? Well, they have. Mice and Marriage is the third book in the Love's Infestation Series.

CHAPTER ONE

The scream coming from the converted warehouse, as Turner snapped the bike lock closed, made him jump to his feet and run to the wide open garage door. He grabbed the auto-release knife handle from the sleeve of his black leather jacket but didn't depress the trigger. Pausing, he peeked around the edge of the door to survey the large open area before he entered. He slipped the knife back into its pocket and pressed the Velcro closed. He wouldn't need it.

Walking in, he sauntered over to the picnic table the young woman was standing on. The thin plastic tablecloth was bunched around her feet as she turned around several times while he approached. Dressed in blue jeans, red wool pea coat, with her hair covered by a white knit hat, she looked to be in her late twenties. She was pretty but not stunning. She reminded him a bit of someone, but he couldn't think who.

"Looking for something?" Turner asked as he neared the table.

Her eyes, big and round, spied him and became wider. She was surprised to see him. "A mouse. There was this huge mouse." She spread her arms wide apart.

Turner, who had seen mice and rats all over the world hadn't ever seen one that large, so he merely grinned. "Afraid of mice?" He stuck his hands in his jacket pockets. The early November day was chilly, and the open garage door made the room the same temperature as the outside. It wasn't an issue while he was riding, but tucking his hands away felt good.

"Have you ever had one crawl up the inside of your pant leg? It's a horrible feeling," she said.

Turner was familiar with the experience and not eager to repeat it, but in a renovated warehouse, now used for events, in an urban area that wasn't likely. Being the gentleman that he was, he figured it was up to him to aid the lady in distress.

He stood next to the picnic table and was now looking up at her. From his jacket pocket, Turner pulled the Velcro straps he wore at his ankles, controlling his pant legs as he biked if he weren't dressed in riding clothes. Today, he had on jeans. He'd removed the straps and put them in his pocket just before he locked his bike.

"These will keep the mice from crawling up your pant legs, though I'm not sure one that large could get up them anyway." Turner wrapped each pant leg with a strap around her ankle. Slim ankle. Shapely leg too, he noticed as he helped her down to the concrete floor. "I think you might not want to use this tablecloth." He picked it up and shook out the wadded mess her feet had made. There were wrinkles and tears over most of it.

"Um, no, I suppose not." She bit her lip, then began to laugh. "You must think I'm pretty ridiculous. My scream probably gave the mouse a heart attack."

"Very likely. He's probably in the next county by now running from you, scared for his life." Turner smiled and held out his hand. "Turner Metcalf, at your service."

"Oh, I'm Noelle Copeland." She held out her gloved hand, and he took it, holding on a bit longer than necessary as he shook it. "Metcalf? Are you... Yes, you're Kyria Jenner's brother. I remember you now from the wedding."

"That's right. I was there. I don't remember you though, and I'm sure I would if we'd met."

A sadly shadowed expression crossed her face. "I kept a pretty low profile that day. Going through a rough patch in my life." The smile she gave was forced, he could tell. "Better times now."

Turner wondered what the rough patch was but didn't ask. Two reasons crossed his mind. First, it was none of his business, and second, he wanted her to smile again.

The chirp of his phone took his focus away from Noelle. Checking the message, he said, "That's from Kyria. She's going to be late. Some decision about the house construction."

The smile he'd wanted to see on Noelle's face returned. "That's happened a lot lately. I was so happy they moved here to Benton when Mark got the job at the hospital. I really like your sister. She's becoming a good friend. I wish we could spend more time together, but between my work and the boys, Kyria starting her decorating business and building their house, finding that time has been tough. I get to see them at Hutch's or the Jenners' but not often enough. At church some, too."

Noelle took the tablecloth from him and moved to toss it in the large black bag lined garbage can. Turner saw a pile of bags with more tablecloths and opened one, pulling the plastic sheet out. Together, they began covering the table after she wiped it down with a wet rag.

"So, this event is a Harvest Hop? Not exactly sure what that is," Turner said. He had a general idea, but figured the topic would lead to more conversation.

"The church holds it every year for the children of the church and the area. It's a way to do some outreach. Maybe get some families to see the reasons behind Thanksgiving and Christmas, rather than just pigging out and buying presents. There are games and races and food, of course. A hayrack ride. They used to have an apple dunking, but too many kids got too wet doing it. Hutch gives a short talk about priorities and such. It's fun. My boys love the quarter hunt."

"Quarter hunt?"

"Yeah, they'll spread a couple of bales of hay out on the driveway and mix a few rolls of quarters in them, separated of course. Then, the kids dive in and hunt for the quarters. They divide the kids up into age groups. They love it. Get all itchy with hay in their clothes, but my boys don't care."

She'd mentioned her boys several times. Was she married? Turner glanced at her left hand. She wore no gloves as she worked with the slippery plastic. Her left hand had no rings, but when she reached to give him a corner, he could see where a set had been; the indent was still faintly there.

Now he had a clue as to what the rough patch was. Noelle's marriage had broken up. Not that long ago either.

"You have boys? How many?" They spread the cloth on the table and began another.

"I have two boys, Camden, who's six and in first grade, and Mace, who's four and in preschool." She smiled as she told him, then it faded. "They're with their dad this weekend. I'm hoping he brings them tomorrow."

"You don't sound very optimistic about the prospect."

"I'm not. Ever since Brad decided his girlfriend was more in tune with his needs, he hasn't been really keen on going to church sponsored events."

Turner could empathize with that. He wasn't necessarily too interested in church events either, although with the pretty young woman standing at the other end of the table smoothing the plastic tablecloth, he might just enjoy one. Or more.

~~~~~

Noelle moved to the next table and tore open the package to release another table cover. There was a lot to do before the Harvest Hop tomorrow. Unfortunately, none of the rest of her committee had shown up to help. Not unusual. They knew she'd do it all, so they weren't very faithful in getting their responsibilities done. Then they'd show up for the accolades when the event went well. Seemed to be the story of her life. Doing everything and getting little credit for it but all the blame if things went wrong.

She flipped the plastic cloth open across the table. The man who'd come to her 'rescue' grabbed it, and helped straighten the orange plastic as it floated to the surface. He was broad shouldered, maybe a little over six feet. His black leather jacket looked to be tailored to exactly fit his body. There were pockets, both zipper and patch, on the front, and sleeves. When he turned to walk to a different table, she thought there might be one on the center of the back. What could be in that one?

He had a biker physique, lean hips, and slim muscular legs. Brown hair with streaks of blonde definitely reminded Noelle of his sister's. It was a bit longer than was popular at the moment, and a bit on the shaggy side. It looked as if it were styled intentionally messy. There was a light beard, or maybe it was just that he hadn't shaved in a few days.

"That's the last of the tablecloths. What else needs to be done?" Turner asked.

Noelle pulled her focus from his shape and clothing, and they began setting up the serving table and coffee pots. They worked in silence for a bit.

"Hey," Noelle said. "I know I was a bit, um, distracted when you came in, but I didn't hear you drive up."

"That's because I didn't. I biked. Was just locking it when you screamed bloody murder."

While they chatted, she leaned down, removed the ankle straps and handed them to him. The comment made her laugh. "I did, didn't I? I'm pretty afraid of mice. Dirty, nasty creatures need to stay out of my path."

Turner joined her laughing.

"You really biked up here in this cold?" She placed a box of plastic spoons next to the one with forks. "That's a long hill."

"It's not that cold. Or at least it wasn't this afternoon.

Kyria's going to take me back to her place. I don't like riding at night. That's why we were meeting here. I knew I wouldn't get back to her place until after dark. Glad we decided on that. I got to meet you, or should I say, rescue you from a gigantic rodent?"

"You're never going to let me live that down, are you?"

He grinned devilishly at her. "Most likely not."

"Well then, I might just have to put you to work tomorrow night, too. Looks like we've done all the damage we can tonight." They walked to the garage door, and she smacked the button to make it close. "Since Kyria's not here to pick you up, how are you going to get to her place? It's dark."

"I was hoping you'd offer to haul me and my bike."

"I don't have a bike rack, and it's a small SUV."

He opened the main door and stepped back to allow her to precede him through. "It'll fit. It folds up pretty small."

Noelle watched as Turner unlocked the bike, pulled a couple of pins, undid some clamps, and folded the lime green bike to the size of a spare tire. "That's pretty sweet. You can put it in almost any car trunk."

"Mostly. Doesn't fit in a Jag or Corvette trunk, among other small sports cars. I've tried. I do have a case so it can be checked luggage when I fly. It's been all over the world with me."

Noelle was getting the idea that Turner just might be out of her economic status. Something about his casual attitude about traveling the world gave her a bit of a clue. She remembered Hutch saying Kyria was rather wealthy with an inheritance from her parents, and it seemed Turner was, too.

"I can give you a lift to Kyria's place, then." Noelle pressed the remote to unlock her car.

"Sweet. I'll text my sister and let her know she doesn't have to come get me." Turner pulled out his cell phone and spent some time pressing the keypad. The swoosh sound indicated delivery, then a few seconds later the phone chirped in reply. "She says great and that you can stay for supper. There's enough for you and the boys."

Turner opened the end gate and carefully laid the folded bike in the back. They got in and, after buckling the seat belts, Noelle started the car.

"Just me, but I'll take her up on the meal. Not often I get a home cooked meal I didn't cook or contribute heavily to."

Turner texted again, presumably to let Kyria know there would only be one more rather than three for supper. Then, silence reigned as they wove through town.

"You mentioned work," Turner broke the quiet. "What and where?"

"I'm a nurse at the Benton Medical Center Urgent Care Clinic. It has regular hours and no swing shifts. Makes it easier as a single parent. I prefer hospital floor nursing, but the twelve-hour shifts and odd weekends make it difficult. I switched to the clinic when Brad left."

They traveled the rest of the way in silence, but not an uncomfortable one. That surprised her. Usually, when she first met someone, any silence made her nervous. Sitting next to Turner didn't. It felt natural.

Soon, they were turning into Kyria and Mark's driveway. They lived in the rental house they'd moved into when Mark took the head hospitalist job at Benton Medical Center. They'd begun planning their house then. Mark's family owned a construction company so it had jumped to the beginning of the list and was now enclosed, and work would continue throughout the winter. They hoped to move in sometime in the spring.

Almost before Noelle put the car in park, Turner was opening the door and jumping out. He got his bike out of the back and escorted Noelle to the front door. He didn't bother to knock, instead unlocked the door and went on in. That made Noelle nervous until she remembered he was living with them while he was in town.

"Hey, Kyria, Mark," Turner yelled as he placed his folded bike in the closet beside the door. "We're here." He took Noelle's coat and hung it up beside his.

Mark appeared in the doorway to the kitchen. The foyer was only a tiled area in front of the door. There was a large living room with a modern, white leather sofa, two blue, upholstered wingback chairs and a glass coffee table to the left. A huge TV hung on the wall facing the couch. Light blue draperies hung at the large picture window. There were shelving units of dark brown wood flanking the window.

Noelle knew Kyria was an interior designer, but this room always looked as if it were a conglomeration of styles trying to fill the space. She was no whiz at decorating, but this just didn't quite work.

She remembered when Mark laughed at the look on her face the first time she's been to their place. "We just combined our furniture for now. Once the house gets finished, some of our things will move to it, and others won't continue as our possessions. We know it doesn't work well, but it's what we have. Kyria cringes every time she comes in here."

"You brought my wayward brother home, I see. I know, I know. This room is awful," Kyria laughed as she entered wiping her hands on a tea towel. "It definitely doesn't do my career as a designer any good, so I don't bring clients here."

"Oh no, did I grimace at the decor again?" Noelle laughed along with Mark and Turner.

"Let's just say your expression didn't exhibit delight at the vision of decorating splendor spreading out before you." Turner's mocking tone earned him a smack on the shoulder by his sister.

CHAPTER TWO

Turner parked his Porsche Macan crossover in the lot, and sat looking at the building overflowing with adults and children. He was surprised at the number of people who had come to the Harvest Hop. He'd thought they'd be lucky to get two dozen, even though he and Noelle had covered that many picnic tables. There were more than three times that number of cars on this side of the building. The lot on the other side had been just as crowded. He wondered if he'd be able to find not only Noelle, but his sister and brother-in-law too.

Turner checked the pockets of his leather jacket. Tucking his phone into one, he got out and headed to the party.

Music played over loudspeakers. The rhythm was something you could dance to. As he listened, it became clear the lyrics weren't typical to what was played on most radio stations. These words lifted up the Lord. Well that was to be expected, he supposed. This was a church event after all.

Like the evening before, the garage door was open, allowing easy movement to and from the building.

Turner moved to the far edge of the entrance and stood looking over the crowd. His six-foot two-inch height gave him an advantage as he could see over most of the people. There she was, standing next to a man who was smiling and chatting with a pretty woman. He looked familiar, but Turner couldn't place where he'd seen him.

The man lifted a microphone to his mouth and said, "In about five minutes, we'll start the first quarter hunt with the three and four-year-olds. It'll be held out the east door, so head on out that way."

A general exodus began, causing Turner to take a couple of steps back to get even further out of the way. Boys and girls of various heights dragged adults by the hand, eager to be the first out the door.

With about half of the crowd now outside, Turner walked across the room to where Noelle was setting more refreshments out onto the serving table.

"Hey," he said.

"Oh, hi. I wasn't sure you were going to make it. Here." She handed him a tray of sandwiches, then picked up another of cut up vegetables. "Help me do this. Then, I'll have a few minutes to chat." They took the trays to another table, and she arranged them, picking up the empty trays. They took them back to the preparation area and handed them off to others to be refilled. "There, I'm done for a bit. Come on, you want to watch the quarter hunt?"

Turner grinned. "Sure. Maybe I'll see if I can find some."

"Nope, you're too old. Only those twelve and younger can participate. My boys will be in the thick of things though." Noelle grabbed his hand and pulled him along behind her. "I know the best place to watch."

They crossed to the exterior wall and went up a small flight of steps. Noelle opened the door and stepped out onto a small balcony overlooking the event.

While Noelle watched the three and four-year-olds rummage through the straw scattered on the pavement, Turner watched her. Only average height, she exuded delight at seeing the children's excitement when they found a quarter. Dressed again in the white stocking cap and red pea coat, she made him think of Christmas. Maybe it was her sparkling green eyes that added that last touch to complete the holiday image.

"There, that's Mace." She pointed to a boy in a blue and green parka. He was holding up a quarter in each hand. When he saw that she had noticed, he stuffed them in his pocket and dove back into the straw.

"Don't you want to be down there with him?" Turner asked.

"Not at the moment. Brad is there. I'd just as soon avoid him whenever possible. At least he brought the boys." Noelle's voice had lost a bit of its enthusiasm.

Turner thought to ask which one he was, but decided to observe. He'd figure it out soon enough. A whistle blew signaling the end to the hunt, and the children ran to the parents who were standing around watching.

Yes, that's the father, Turner thought, as Mace ran over to a dark haired man who had his arm around a young woman. She was pretty enough, but seemed ill at ease. She didn't speak to Mace, who was pulling quarters out of his pocket to show his father. Another boy, a little older than Mace, had on a yellow and blue coat. He patted Mace on the shoulder and said a few words.

More quarters were scattered in the straw and raked in. When the next heat was announced, the older boy raced forward, diving into the straw. A quick glance back at the father and young woman showed her leaning close, holding her phone at arm's length, taking a selfie.

When the whistle blew, Noelle said, "Come on. I want to speak with the boys." She grabbed his hand and pulled him back into the building, down the stairs, and out into the night air. They met her boys who hugged her. She dropped his hand to embrace her sons.

"Mommy, I got seven quarters," Mace said.

"I got nine," the other one announced.

"Wonderful. Do you want me to put them in your room? You can have them when you get home tomorrow."

"Sure." They handed their treasures over, and Noelle tucked them into her coat pocket.

"You remember our deal. One quarter goes into the toys fund at church next week." She rubbed each boy's head, knocking their stocking hats askew.

"Yep. We remember," the oldest one said.

"You're really going to, like, make them give a quarter to some, like, toy fund?" It was the young woman standing next to the boys' father who spoke. Her gum snapped as she spoke.

"Some kids don't have parents who can buy them stuff for Christmas. This helps them out," Mace said.

"Yeah, I don't mind. I'd rather give them one of my quarters than keep it, if they aren't going to get anything for Christmas."

Turner was surprised that such young children were willing to give rather than receive. The look the other woman gave showed she didn't understand the sentiment. He glanced at Noelle. The pride on her face was evident. She deserved to be proud. She'd instilled a spirit of generosity in her sons that was missing in many adults.

"Brad, Kim, this is Turner Metcalf. He's Kyria Jenner's brother." Noelle waved a hand toward him. "Turner, these are Brad Copeland and Kimberly Renford."

Turner extended his hand, and Brad shook it. Kim looked bored.

"You guys did real well in the quarter hunt," Turner said. He extended one hand to each boy who clasped it to shake. "I'm Turner."

"I'm Camden."

"I'm Mason, but you can call me Mace."

"Wow," both boys said as Turner released their hands. He'd left two quarters in each hand.

"One of those goes into the toy fund," Turner instructed. "You can keep the other one."

"Thanks." The gratitude was expressed as the coins were shoved into pockets.

"Come on, boys." Noelle laid a hand on each boy's shoulder. "Let's go get you something to eat before you head back to your dad's for the night."

As the boys ran ahead, Brad said, "About that, Noelle. Would you mind if they went home with you? Kim and I wanted to go out after we're finished here."

"Yeah, there's, like, this new movie out this weekend. We, like, want to go see it." Kim snapped her gum.

"Well, I, like, don't mind having my sons with me." Noelle's gaze shifted from Kim to Brad. "Just don't be asking for them on my weekends. You don't want them now, so don't expect them then."

Brad just nodded.

"How soon can we, like, leave, Braddy? I don't want to be, like, late to the show." Kim hung onto Brad's arm.

"Let's go tell the boys about the change of plans," Brad wrapped an arm around Kim's waist. "Good to meet you, Tucker," Brad said, holding out his other hand to shake again.

"You too, Brant. Have fun at your movie."

"It's Brad," the man said.

"Yes, like, I know. Mine's Turner."

~~~~~

Noelle clapped a hand over her mouth. She wasn't going to laugh until Brad and Kim were out of ear shot. "How did you pick up on how Brad is so fast? He's done that same thing to people ever since I've known him. He messes up their name, making them tell him again."

"It's common enough. He's trying to claim dominance. He's inferring that I'm not important enough for him to remember my name. I just turned it back on him. It's, like, no big deal." Turner's voice rose in imitation of Kim on the last sentence.

Noelle did lose it then, breaking out laughing. "Come on. Let's go find my sons. I need to be Mom now, as well as head pooh-bah of this shindig."

They were seated at a table with Chloe and Hutch. Chloe held baby Noah, who was grabbing for whatever he could reach. At ten-months-old, whatever he was able to grasp went straight to his mouth.

"Hey," Noelle said. "What do you think, guys? You get to sleep in your own beds tonight." She looked at her sons. They didn't seem too upset that they weren't going to be at their father's place.

"It's cool. We don't do much at Dad's anyway. Mostly play video games," Camden said. Mace just nodded.

It broke her heart to know Brad wasn't paying attention to his sons. Even though she never wanted him back, Noelle wanted a positive relationship between her ex-husband and the boys. She exchanged a glance with Chloe. One of Noelle's best friends, she, Chloe, and Whitney had grown up together and their closeness continued. Both Chloe and Whitney had been faithful and supportive during the difficult months surrounding her divorce.

"Turner, you remember my brother, Hutch, and Chloe. Hutch married Kyria and Mark. Man, it's hard to believe that was a year and a half ago."

Hutch had stood and was shaking hands with Turner.

"Now I know why you looked familiar," Turner said. "I knew I recognized you from somewhere when I came in earlier." He looked at Noelle. "You two do look like siblings. More than Kyria and I do."

"Yeah, I got all the looks." Everyone turned to look at the speaker. It was Kyria, with Mark trailing behind.

"Hey, did I see Brad and the bimbo leaving?" Mark asked.

"Hush, Mark. Not in front of..." Noelle pointed to Camden and Mace.

"Oops, sorry."

Noelle didn't think Mark looked very apologetic.

"You getting reacquainted?" Kyria looked at her brother, and made a circle with her hand encompassing all the adults.

Discussion turned general, with Noelle attending to her hosting duties, and Hutch periodically making announcements. Then, he spoke to the crowd, telling that the reason for the holiday season was about having gratitude for God's bountiful provision, which culminated in the life, death, and resurrection of his Son. After Hutch concluded, the party began to break up.

Noelle sat the boys at a table, telling them to be good while she helped with the cleanup. When she came back to fetch them, Noelle found Turner seated between them with a deck of cards in his hands.

"Mommy, did you know Turner can do card tricks?" Camden asked.

"Yeah, they're awesome." Mace looked up at Noelle, excitement on his face.

"He said he'd teach us how to do them. Can he, Mom?" Camden asked, the same enthusiasm in his voice.

Noelle looked at Turner. There was a slightly boyish smile on his handsome face. Also, a touch of sheepishness, as if he knew he'd been manipulating her sons to be able to spend more time with her.

"Sure he can. Right after he treats us all to lunch after church tomorrow. We'll meet you right before Sunday school. It starts at nine." Noelle saw Turner's eyes widen just a bit, but his smile never wavered.

"Sounds like a plan to me. What do you say, guys?" Turner shifted his gaze between the boys on either side of him. Mace climbed into his lap.

"Hurray. I can't wait to show Uncle Hutch the trick. He'll be surprised."

As they left, Noelle noticed Turner unzip a pocket on the upper sleeve of his jacket and tuck the deck of cards inside. "You keep a deck of cards on you all the time?"

He grinned at her. "You'd be surprised what I have on me at all times."

CHAPTER THREE

Kyria was surprised, no shocked, when Turner was up and dressed in khakis and an Irish wool sweater on Sunday morning. Her mouth dropped open when he stated he was going to church. Not only church, but Sunday school.

She placed her hand on his forehead. "You sure you're not sick?"

Turner batted her hand away. "No, Noelle invited me. Then we're going out to lunch, and I'm going to teach Camden and Mace some card tricks. Don't know how well they'll manage with such small hands, but they're interested and…"

"It gives you a chance to be with Noelle." Kyria drew her eyebrows together. "Don't mess with her affections, Turner. She's a wonderful mother and woman. She didn't deserve what Brad did to her."

"Besides, Chloe and Whitney would take you down faster than you can spit if you hurt her," Mark said, coming up behind Kyria. "I might too, and I know Hutch would."

"Not to worry. I don't plan to. I like her and the boys."

"Just know," Kyria said. "You've been warned. You have a tendency to disappear for months and even years at a time."

"Look, I know I've been pretty absent in the past. I'm changing. Taking on more of a role in the businesses. Doing some of the tasks Uncle Russ did.

"Sure, I'll still be traveling some, but it will be for business. A few days here and there. I'm thinking of getting a place here in Benton. Maybe an apartment or condo. That way I could be more of a brother." Turner wrapped his arm around Kyria's shoulders. "I know I've been pretty bad at it for a long time. I want us to have more of a permanent relationship. You and I are all we have as family, not counting Mark. I want to be part of your lives."

Kyria looked at him with hope in her eyes. It made his heart ache to know he'd hurt her with his absence. It couldn't be helped though. Soon, it should all come to a close.

Turner squeezed her into a hug. "Hey, I might even allow you to practice your interior decorating on my place. You can certainly use it. This place doesn't say much for your skills."

~~~~~

Turner was standing in the church lobby with Kyria and Mark when Noelle and her sons entered. He walked over and fist bumped each boy. "Hey, guys. Good to see you again. Have you decided where we're going to eat lunch?"

"We get to choose?" Camden asked.

"Yep, I don't know all that many restaurants in town. I'm counting on you to take me to the best place you know."

"Other than fast food," Noelle interjected.

"Yeah, Sunday's not for burgers and fries, unless it's more upscale." Turner winked.

"Head on to your classrooms. You don't want to be late." Noelle waved a hand, and her sons took off. "Walk."

Kyria and Mark had moved to stand next to Turner. Noelle and his sister hugged a greeting. "How'd you get my brother to come to church today? I've been asking him to come ever since he moved in with us."

Noelle grinned sheepishly. "I bribed him with going out to lunch with us afterwards. Sort of made it a prerequisite. If he wanted to teach the boys the card tricks they were begging to learn, he had to join us for church and Sunday school. Oh, and treat us to lunch, too."

"Don't think that would have worked for you," Mark said, squeezing his wife with his arm around her shoulder.

Turner was only half listening to the conversation. He was looking at Noelle. Instead of the red pea coat, she had on a long dark gray, double breasted, wool coat that flared at the bottom. She began unbuttoning it, so he helped her take it off and stepped away to hang it up as she murmured her thanks. Her voice was soft and low and did weird things to his insides. Or maybe breakfast just wasn't sitting well in his stomach.

"Come on. Let's go head to Liam's class. It's pretty deep, but I hope you'll enjoy it. We've been in the book of John for— I don't know how long." Noelle waved for the Jenners to lead the way.

Following her down the hall, Turner watched the sway of her hips. She was dressed in a colorful tunic and black leggings. Knee high black boots encased her slim legs. That weird feeling, it definitely had something to do with Noelle, rather than his breakfast.

As they entered the classroom she said, "Liam's a great teacher. We dig really deep into the Scriptures."

Turner found out that was true. Liam's teaching style was relaxed, and the knowledge he had of the ancient culture of Israel was vast. Discussion was encouraged, and many in the class added insights he'd never considered of the verses they went over.

Mamie, his and Kyria's nanny, had taken them to church, but since his family had traveled to various parts of the world so often the services varied greatly, not only in style and denomination, but also in language. Under Mamie's influence and continual teaching, he learned of his need for the Savior and had accepted when he was about twelve.

When he had left home for Oxford at barely the age of seventeen, his interest in pursuing his faith diminished. The cares and concerns of college life, and the interests of a young man, pulled him away. Then, a couple of events had instilled doubts and sent his life in a different direction. Turner wasn't sure he was interested in renewing his faith, but he definitely was in getting to know Noelle better.

~~~~~

The boys wanted spaghetti, so they went to Bonacelli's Italian Garden, inviting Mark and Kyria along. The Jenners declined, as they wanted to go over to the construction site of their new home, and inspect what had been completed this past week.

When Turner pulled the door of the restaurant open, the aroma of garlic, herbs, and yeasty bread made his mouth water and his stomach growl. He agreed with Mace's comment that he thought heaven smelled like this.

As they followed the hostess to their table, Noelle stopped beside a woman in a wheelchair. "Whitney, oh I'm so glad to see you. I haven't had time to come see you since you got home. How are you doing?" A handsome man of similar age to Turner, and an older woman were also at the table.

"As well as can be expected, they tell me. It's slow going. Mom says I need to just let time heal all the wounds." Her left arm was in a cast, and by the angle the wheelchair was at the table, Turner could see her left leg was, too.

"Turner, I'd like to introduce you to Whitney, her mother, Emily Houston, and Dr. Keith Austin. Whitney was in a work accident about a month ago," Noelle said.

"Hi, Keith. We've met before. He's a friend and colleague of Mark's. Nice to meet you, Emily, Whitney. Sorry to hear about your mishap. I hope you'll heal quickly and with little pain."

"Hey, Whitney," Camden said. "Can I sign my name on your cast?" He was studying it. There were several names and drawings on both her arm and leg casts.

"Sure, Cam. Let me get the markers." Whitney began digging in the purse on her lap.

Turner spoke with the hostess and was shown which table they would occupy, while Camden and Mace both signed the leg and arm casts. Whitney was telling Noelle how much she was missing going to church. Keith would come over each Sunday morning, and they'd watch the service stream online.

Once the signing, and Mace's drawing of a dog with lots of black spots was complete, they went to their table and were soon placing their orders.

While they waited for their salads to arrive, Turner's phone rang. The ringtone identified the caller. "I have to take this. Please excuse me." He got up and hurried outside, sliding his finger across the screen as he went, to connect the call. This was not a complication he wanted right now. There weren't supposed to be any events until after the holidays.

Outside, he stepped around to the far side of the restaurant, away from anyone who might overhear. "Yes."

"Sorry, I know we thought there would be a delay, but I need you at an event in Monaco on Friday, then in Tel Aviv on Saturday."

Turner bit back a curse. He struggled with his irritation at the interruption of his plans to get to know Noelle better. Leaving for several days wasn't going to endear him to her, especially since he couldn't totally explain why and where he'd be going.

"Okay, I guess the sooner this is completed, the better. Send me the details and arrangements. You know where I am?"

"Always. Your flight leaves at five-thirty Thursday morning."

"Lovely."

The caller chuckled. "I know how you like the early flights."

"Yeah, right."

~~~~~

Noelle could tell Turner wasn't pleased with whatever the call had concerned. There was something about his demeanor that was not only displeased, but totally different. It was as if a different person were approaching the table. The loose, relaxed man was gone, and one of tightly controlled intensity walked in his place.

"Is everything all right?" She asked, as Turner sat down.

He sat staring at his salad, then looked at her. "Yes and no. Yes, everything is fine, and no because I have to go on a business trip early Thursday. I won't get back until at least Sunday evening if not Monday."

"Oh, I thought you independently wealthy people didn't have to work." She grinned at him and took a bite of salad.

"That may be true, but someone has to look after the businesses that keep the independently wealthy people independent and wealthy. I've started taking over some of those responsibilities. The lawyer who handles the trusts for Kyria and me has been doing it. Kyria made it clear she thinks I'm slacking by letting him do it all."

"Are you?" Noelle eyed him. Yes, she was attracted to him, but if he were simply a narcissist, she'd be done with him before they started.

"To an extent, she was accurate. I have let him deal with the vast majority of the work. Other things kept me from taking more of a role. Now, those duties are coming to a close, so I'll be more active in all the businesses."

"What sort of things?" He seemed to be offering information, but details were lacking.

Turner looked at the boys who were listening intently. He grinned. "I'm an international spy who's involved in a plot to overthrow an evil regime that's taken over a country, killed a lot of people and doesn't care about anything but power and money." He shrugged, and the relaxed persona settled around him like a mantle. "If I tell you more, well, I'll just have to kill you."

"Really?" Mace's eyes were wide with awe and a little fear.

Turner laughed, tousled his hair. "Nope, just thought it was fun to say." He forked a bite of tomato into his mouth.

CHAPTER FOUR

Turner rang the doorbell and waited for it to be answered. It was Tuesday, and he was bringing pizza for supper to Noelle and her boys. They'd had such a good time on Sunday. At least he had. After eating they'd gone back to Noelle's house. Turner had spent the afternoon teaching card tricks. The boys' hands were too small to do the tricks smoothly, but he and Noelle had cheered and been amazed when they performed them.

The door opened, and Camden yelled over his shoulder, "Turner's here with the pizza."

"Well, let him in and close the door. We're not trying to heat the outside," Noelle said from another room.

"Come on." Camden closed the door, and led the way to the kitchen.

As they went, Turner reviewed his surroundings. To the left was a room littered with toys. Legos were scattered on the tan carpeting, as were some action figures and various size vehicles. They moved on into a great room. In the center was a dark green L-shaped sofa, with a square oak coffee table in front. A huge flat screen TV was mounted on the wall to the right. The wall he was facing was filled with large glass French doors that led to a covered porch. A desk with a computer sat to the left of the doors.

"Hey," Noelle's voice pulled his attention from the house to her. She was standing behind an island in the open kitchen. Mace sat on a barstool counting out napkins from a stack.

Turner walked over and placed the pizza boxes on the counter, not taking his eyes off her. She looked lovely. Her honey blonde hair was in loose waves around her shoulders.

"A bit chilly?" he asked.

"Huh?"

"Your sweatshirt." He grinned. "I'm freakin' cold?"

"Oh," Noelle looked down at the words on her navy sweatshirt. "I was when I got home."

"I gots eight napkins, Mommy." Mace held up the white paper squares.

"Great, I've got the plates. Let's eat."

Mace scrambled down from the stool, raced around the sofa, and slammed the napkins on the coffee table. "Can we watch The LEGO Movie?"

"Sure, find the DVD, but let Camden put it in." Noelle rounded the island carrying plates. "Last time Mace tried, the DVD ended up scratched."

Camden was bringing bottled water when Turner placed the pizza boxes on the table. Soon, the boys were settled on the floor around the coffee table with plates of cheese pizza. Noelle was curled up in the corner of the sofa with supreme, and Turner had pieces of both kinds.

Turner watched the boys and Noelle more than he watched the movie. The closeness between them, and relaxed atmosphere attracted him. While he was growing up that hadn't been his experience. Strict rules and careful cultivation of appropriate demeanor was the norm. Whenever he had seen his parents, formality was expected. They would never have allowed him to sit on the floor while eating a meal. Eating took place in the dining room, using the correct utensils.

Although Turner believed his parents loved him and Kyria, they didn't demonstrate it outwardly. Being expected to learn how to deal with the businesses began when Turner was Camden's age. Only with Mamie was Turner able to relax and receive the love she wanted to lavish on him.

By the time the movie was over, Noelle was asleep. Turner shushed the boys and led them, on tiptoe, across the carpet, into the room by the front door with toys scattered across the floor. He cleared a space and sat down.

"Did you like the movie?" Mace asked. "It's my favorite. Look." Mace picked up a LEGO construction. "I made this all by myself."

"Pretty snazzy there, bud." Turner had no clue what it was. The next few minutes were taken up with both boys showing him all sorts of things they'd built with the little blocks.

"Hey, guys," Turner said. "You like to play little jokes on your mom?"

"Yeah," they both said loudly. Turner placed his finger by his lips. "Shush, we don't want her waking up. Next question. Can you keep a secret?"

Camden's enthusiasm dimmed. "Mom said there are some secrets we aren't supposed to keep."

"That's right. Very good for you to remember." He

ruffled the dark head of hair. "This isn't one of those kind. This is more to tease your mom a little bit when I'm not here"

"You going somewhere?" asked Mace.

"Well, home after a while. I don't live here, you know." Turner grinned. The thought that he'd like to live there dove into his head.

"Oh, yeah."

Turner pulled several small gray furry cones out of his pocket. He held one up. There were two pink felt circles folded and stuck on behind two black beads sewn near the tip, which had a pink pompon. A gray piece of yarn extended from the base.

"It's a mouse," Mace said as he took one.

Camden took another one, his eyes studying it for a moment then, eyes sparkling with glee, he looked at Turner and said. "Mommy's afraid of mice." The smile on his face made it clear he knew what was being proposed.

Turner's eyes twinkled with delight. "Yeah. How about we tease her about it?"

"How?" Mace asked.

"Well, first, do you have a place to hide these little guys? Someplace your mom won't look and find them?"

The boys looked around the room. Camden jumped up and went to a book bag in the corner. "In here. It's my bag from last year. We keep crayons and markers in it. As long as we keep them picked up, Mommy won't look in it."

Turner looked at the bricks, cars, and action figures all over the floor. "You sure you can do that?"

"Yeah, these are from today. We'll put them away

before we go to bed. Mommy makes us." Camden stuck the mice way down in the bag.

"Friday, one of you put one somewhere she might find it. Don't laugh or point or giggle. That will give it away. Then maybe a couple days later hide another one for her to find. You think you can figure out where to hide them?"

Both boys nodded solemnly.

"Okay, then. How about this? We'll sneak in and put the mouse right where she will see it when she wakes up. Then, we'll pick up in here. We'll stay in here until she comes or screams, which ever is first."

Both boys giggled.

"Now, we have to be totally quiet so we don't wake her up. If we do, it's all done for."

"We need to be as quiet as a spy." Camden looked at Mace. "Know what I mean?"

"Yeah, shush."

Turner took point, and led the way from the room and down the hall to the great room. Noelle was still sound asleep on the sofa. He turned around and motioned for them to follow and be quiet. They stopped at the end of the sofa, and Turner moved along the back. Where two cushions came together on the back, he tucked the mouse between, with its nose and ears sticking out. He looked at the boys, and they nodded, grinning. Mace covered his mouth with his hands. They backed away and fled down the hall back to their play room.

They'd picked up all the bricks and action figures, and were zooming cars around, when a scream came from the other room. Camden and Mace rolled on the floor laughing. Turner smiled and fell over between them.

~~~~~

Noelle opened her eyes. How long had she been asleep? She glanced over the back of the sofa, to check the clock on the kitchen wall, and screamed. She nearly said a word she'd wash her boys' mouths out with soap if they used it.

Grabbing the furry little rodent as she leaped from the sofa, Noelle followed the sound of laughter, stomping to the play room. Turner was lying on the floor with Camden and Mace, mauling him as they all laughed. It stopped her anger totally.

Here was a man she'd met four days ago, laughing and playing with her sons in abandon. Brad hadn't done that ever, that she could remember. He'd come home from work, strip down to his underwear or lounge pants, and park himself in front of the TV. If either boy tried to get him to play, he'd tell them he was too tired. Maybe that was true. It never took Brad long to fall asleep after supper.

"Oh, so you think that was funny, huh?" Noelle tried to keep her tone harsh and her lips from twitching, but it was hard.

"Yeah, Mommy," Mace jumped up and grabbed her around the waist. "You screamed really loud." With that, he fell down again on top of Turner, who wrapped an arm around him and began a knuckle rub on his head.

"Well, if you think you're going to get this mouse back, mister, you've got another think coming."

CHAPTER FIVE

Turner slid into the driver's seat of the Macan, and glanced at Noelle as he buckled his seatbelt. Since the boys were with their father on Wednesday evenings, he'd asked Noelle to go out to dinner with him. With his flight leaving at such an early hour the next morning, he wouldn't sleep that night. Instead, he planned to spend most of it with Noelle then pack and be at the airport in plenty of time. He'd sleep on the flight. Going first-class made that easy. The seats stretched out into beds. Not the most comfortable beds, but better than sitting up for all those hours.

"I've made reservations at La Maison." Turner pulled away from the curb.

"They actually let you park your purple car at that fancy place?"

"It's iris, not purple, and yes, they even valet park it for me."

"Camden and Mace say your car is purple." There was laughter in Noelle's tone.

"Yeah, I know, but it's iris. You can check online on the Porsche website. Or, I think the window sticker is in the glove compartment. You can see the color on it."

Noelle just laughed. "Defensive about the color of your car much?"

"Mark calls it purple, too."

She laughed again at the disgruntled tone of his voice. "I'll call it iris if it'll make you happy."

Turner chuckled. "Don't do me any favors."

The valet did park the car for them and seemed happy to drive such an expensive vehicle, even if it was purple. They entered the restaurant, and were seated in a small booth tucked into a corner with a round table. A low bowl with freesia blossoms and tea light candles floating in water decorated the table, giving off a pleasing fragrance.

"The scallops here are wonderful, as is the blue-cheese sirloin. My favorite is the porterhouse cajun style," Turner said.

"They all sound wonderful."

"Is that you, Noelle?" A nasal voice interrupted their perusal of the menus.

Turner saw Noelle grimace, then morph her lips into some semblance of a smile.

"It is. I thought it was. See, Jim, I told you it was Noelle Copeland. Now, who is this? I don't think I've seen him before. Are you new in town? Oh, wait, maybe I did see you at church last Sunday. You were with Dr. Mark Jenner and his wife. With the two Dr. Jenners, it's just so confusing. She has that strange name. Kerna? No, Karna, yes, I think that's it. Yes, Karna." The woman flipped a hand at Turner.

Deciding he needed to be polite, Turner stood. "I'm Turner Metcalf, relatively new in town, brother to Kyria Jenner. And you are?"

"This is…" Noelle began.

"I'm Alene, and this is Jim, my husband. We just finished. We come for the early bird special. Get here before five-thirty, and it's twenty-five percent off."

"Noelle, your team did a great job on the Harvest Hop. Jim and me stopped by for a little while. The decorations and all were really great. Tell your team they did a real fine job. I already told Mary Sue how great she did. That's our daughter." She addressed the last comment to Turner. "Well, we need to get going. It was good to meet you, Tanner. Hope to see you again at church some time."

Turner sat down and looked at Noelle. "Did she give their last name?"

"No." Noelle shook her head. "It's Dufflemeyer. Alene and Jim Dufflemeyer."

"Remind me to hide if they are around next time I'm at church."

"Only if you return the favor."

"Does he ever get a chance to speak?"

"I'm not sure. I don't think I've ever heard his voice, now that I think about it."

"Maybe he never gets the chance."

"Probably," Noelle laughed.

They placed their orders, and Turner saw Noelle studying him. "What? Do I have hair growing out my nose?"

"I was just wondering where you're going on your trip? You never said."

"Monte Carlo. There's a charity event I'm going to. It's raising money for relief and medicine to go to Alawanda."

"That's that country in Africa that has that dictator, I forget his name, who has killed so many of the people. I hear there are lots of children left orphans."

"Yes, it's a terrible situation. His name is Demar Atul. Prince Albert of Monaco is hosting the event."

"You're going to see Prince Albert?" Noelle sounded and looked incredulous.

"Well, yes, he'll be there. Whether I have the opportunity to speak with him is a different matter. He'll be busy hosting. I try to always greet the host and thank him or her for the invitation, but sometimes I can only speak with the attaché."

"You get invited to charity events often?"

Their salads arrived, so Turner waited until they were served before answering.

"Quite a few. More since I've taken a more active role in the businesses. Uncle Russ did most of it before, even though I went to many."

"Really?"

"Yeah, they aren't as interesting as you might think. It's usually the same people, talking about the same things. There's the chatter about who's involved with whom that isn't their spouse, what their children are doing, who's in rehab for this or that addiction, who's getting married or divorced. Very little is ever spoken of concerning the charity the money is being raised for. That's not what's important to most of those in attendance. It's the see-and-be-seen and photographed. What website or magazine will they be featured on. That sort of thing."

"Is that what you go for?"

"No, I try to keep as low a profile as I can. Not that I can avoid being photographed some, but I'm not a celebrity and don't want to be. I see how they are hounded by the paparazzi, and want no part of it."

Turner fought down the feeling of panic he always had when he thought of being followed. He picked up his wine glass and was glad to see his hand didn't shake. The sip of Pinot grigio settled his nerves. You'd think after twenty-three years the feelings would lessen.

"If I'm able, I'll take a selfie with the Prince and send it to you. Would you like that? No promises though. It's not quite a high society thing to do, but he might think it's funny to have his photo sent to my girlfriend."

He saw Noelle blush.

"You think I'm your girlfriend?" She looked down at the table. He must have embarrassed her.

"I'd like to think so." Turner took her hand. "I'm very attracted to you, Noelle. I like the boys, too. I get to play with them in ways I never did as a kid. That's fun. But you. You are so very special. You're a wonderful mother. You don't display bitterness over what happened in your marriage. You're giving and generous. You have a sense of humor about most things." He grinned. "You're afraid of mice, even fake ones. What more could a man ask for?"

"You've only known me for six days. How can you know all that?"

"Well, the mice thing— that was revealed even before we met."

Noelle made a dismissive noise.

"I've always been a pretty good judge of character. Plus we've spent several hours on Saturday, all of Sunday, and yesterday together. You saw how I figured out about Alene and Jim Dufflemeyer. How can you doubt that I can know character quickly?"

When Noelle laughed at his last statement, he went

on. "I hate that I have to leave in the morning. I'm afraid this might not be the only event I have to go to over the next few weeks. I especially don't like having to be gone over the weekend. It cuts into the time I could spend with you, Camden, and Mace."

"Yes, the boys are home this weekend. They were disappointed you weren't going to be around to teach them new card tricks and play Legos."

"Hopefully I'll be able to come and play some time next week after school. Can we set up a play date, Mommy?"

"So it's playing with my sons that's the most attractive thing about me, huh?"

"No, ma'am. There's a lot about you that's attractive." Turner allowed his eyes to roam her torso. "Way more attractive than playing with the boys."

~~~~~

Turner zipped the garment bag holding his tuxedo, and placed his shaving kit on top of the other items in his suitcase. He'd checked and rechecked the kit's contents as he normally did. Packing was routine for him. He could practically do it in his sleep.

He glanced at the clock on the nightstand; 1:47. The taxi he'd ordered would be there at 2:30. He'd be early at the airport but knew if he waited here he'd fall asleep. Better to be at the gate asleep than here. He didn't want to miss the flight.

Sitting down on the bed with his back against the headboard, Turner pulled his laptop onto his lap and booted it up. He opened the file with the details of the trip and went over them again. Everything looked in order. Fly to Nice, France. A driver would meet him at the airport and take him to his hotel in Monte Carlo.

The charity event was being held there, making his attendance simple.

Saturday morning he'd be driven back to Nice, where he'd catch his flight to Tel Aviv. There he'd have the meeting. Since the timeframe of that wasn't determined, his return flights hadn't been confirmed. He'd do that once the session in Israel was completed. Turner hoped it could be accomplished quickly. He wanted to get back to Noelle and the boys.

When they'd finished supper, Turner had driven Noelle home. They'd talked about going to a movie. It would have been the late showing, and Noelle had to work the next day. Turner had walked her to the door and declined her invitation to come in. Instead he'd tipped her chin up and lowered his lips to hers. The intent had been for a soft sweet kiss, but that flew from his head the second their mouths touched. Wrapping his arms around Noelle, he drew her against him as he deepened the kiss. When he separated his lips from hers, they were both breathless.

"I think it's a good thing I'm not coming in. I wouldn't want to leave."

"I think you're right. I'm not sure I'd want you to, but I couldn't let you stay."

"No." He'd lowered his head again, and they spent a few more lovely moments tasting the sweetness of each other. Then a dog began barking. "I think that's my signal to leave."

"That's Mr. Kirkland's dog. He'll keep barking until he's let inside. Mr. Kirkland lives straight across the street, and is the biggest gossip in the neighborhood. Unless you want us to be seen kissing, and have it spread all over by 8:30 tomorrow morning, you'd better get back into that purple car and head home."

"It's iris."

Turner smiled at the memory. Yes, he definitely hoped the Tel Aviv meeting was completed in a swift manner. He wanted to be back in Benton as soon as possible.

~~~~~

"Eeek!!" Noelle dropped the toy mouse she'd found in her work shoe. She swiped it up into her hand and stormed out of her bedroom. It was Friday morning, and she was getting ready to take the boys to school and herself to the clinic.

"Who put this in my shoe?" She'd gone into the boys' room and found them giggling. Her angry tone made them quit and stand stiff, looking at her. Their slightly fearful expressions made her stop and think. It wasn't a real mouse. It was a toy. Just because she was afraid of real mice didn't mean she had to fear this little thing. She smiled, which made Camden and Mace relax. "Did Turner give you this to put in my shoe?"

"He didn't say to put it in your shoe. We thought that up by ourselves." Mace looked so pleased at their accomplishment.

"Well, it was a good hiding place. It certainly startled me." Noelle turned to go.

"Mommy, can we have the mouse back?" Camden held out his hand, looking hopeful. "Please?"

"Um, I don't think so. I'll just keep it. Do you have anymore?"

"No. We don't have anymore." Both boys spoke at the same time.

She looked at them. They seemed just a bit too innocent to her.

Back in her room, Noelle placed the mouse on the floor and set her shoe on top of it, pressing down just a bit. The pink nose just peeked out from below. She got her phone and took a picture. *Found this in my shoe. See what happens to mice around here?* She sent the message to Turner's phone.

A couple of minutes later her phone beeped, indicating a new message.

Poor little mouse. He wasn't doing anything wrong. A crying emoji came a second later.

Noelle smiled and finished getting ready for work.

At lunch she checked her phone. There was a message from Turner. It was a photo. Turner standing with Prince Albert and his wife, Princess Charlene, smiling.

When they arrived home that evening, Camden and Mace got a snack and settled around the coffee table doing their homework. Noelle went to put some laundry in the dryer. She opened the door. In the lint trap sat another furry gray mouse. This time she didn't scream, but she did jump a little.

Now she knew what was going on. Turner had given the boys the mice and told them to hide them where she could find them. It also explained the oh-so-innocent looks on her sons' faces. Hopefully, they hadn't outright lied to her that morning when she'd asked if they had any more mice. Maybe they'd already hidden them all, so technically they didn't have any more. It was splitting hairs a little, but she was going to let it pass and play along.

"Eeeek!" Noelle yelled from the door to the laundry room. She heard giggles from the great room. "I thought you guys said you don't have any more of those mice."

"We don't," Camden yelled back.

More giggles.

Yep, they had hidden more mice around the house. Who knew how many she'd find as she went about her routine. She'd have to react to each one. That would delight her boys, which would make her happy.

~~~~~

Turner placed his laptop on the plane seat, and put the bag in the overhead compartment. The last few days had been long and filled. His adjustment to the time zone changes was just now settling in, and he was headed back to the U.S. After they'd fed him, Turner planned to spend the rest of the flight asleep.

Turner buckled in and booted the laptop up. Logging onto the Internet, he emailed Kyria and Noelle that he was on his way back to the States. He wanted to tell Noelle more, but didn't. He logged off and wrote the report of his trip, finishing just as the announcement was made to please turn off all computers in preparation for take-off.

While in Tel Aviv, Turner had gone to a Christian family owned shop, purchasing candy and handmade toys for Camden and Mace. He'd bought a gold chain necklace for Noelle, and another for Kyria for Christmas. On Noelle's he'd put a gold mouse charm. He thought it was cute. It was cartoony, but not a Mickey. Even if she didn't like it, the boys would think it was funny.

Turner sat staring at nothing. Oh, how he wished this entire thing was over. Completed. Successful. It was nearly five years in the making. It seemed like forever. The culmination was approaching. With it they would either accomplish their goal, or everything would come crashing down around them.

"You look tired, Mr. Metcalf," the flight attendant said. "Tough trip?"

Turner looked up at the woman standing in the aisle. She was an attendant he'd seen several times before on various flights. "A quick one. Flew from the States on Thursday morning before anyone should ever be up." He went on to briefly outline being in Monaco, then on to Tel Aviv. He chuckled. "I'm just getting used to the time, and it's time to head across multiple zones again."

"We'll get you fed, and then it's a long flight. You should be able to get some rest."

Turner couldn't stifle a yawn. "I plan to."

CHAPTER SIX

Noelle jerked the front door open, knowing she wasn't looking her most friendly. Frustration ate at her insides. All she needed right now was some solicitor wanting to sell her something, or a charity wanting a donation. Seeing Turner standing there with a bag in his hand swept the feeling away, allowing pleasure to replace it.

"Hi, I'm so glad to see you. How was your trip? Thanks for the photo." Noelle was babbling, and she knew it. She hadn't realized how much she'd missed him over the few days he'd been gone.

"Are you going to invite me in, or shall I just give you these and be on my way?" Turner held out the shopping bag.

"Oh, oh. Of course." Noelle stepped back out of the way, allowing him to enter. Here she was, dressed in her oldest, baggiest, most comfortable, rattiest sweatshirt, and pants with her hair pulled back in a scrunchie.

"Cute slippers," Turner said. His grin was teasing, and Noelle knew her face was turning red.

On her feet were purple elephant slippers. "Camden

and Mace gave them to me for Christmas or my birthday last year. When your birthday is so close to the holiday, you either get one gift for both, or you can't remember what you got for which."

By now they'd reached the great room, and two boys jumped up from the floor and raced over to him, giving Turner a hug. Noelle wasn't sure their becoming so attached to Turner was such a good thing. He was staying in Benton with his sister for the holidays. She didn't want her sons to be hurt when he left after the New Year and forgot all about them.

"I've brought each of you a gift. Nothing big or fancy or expensive." Turner glanced at Noelle as he said the last. He dug into the plastic bag, and pulled out small brown paper bags, and handed one to each boy. Funny, she'd have thought someone as wealthy and well traveled as he would have some fancy tote bag.

"Cool," said Camden. "Thank you. Come on, Mace. Let's give these a try." They ran back to the coffee table and began spinning the wooden tops they each had received.

"Here, you all can share these. I figured you wouldn't want me to give it straight to them."

Noelle took the bag and looked in. There were several bags filled with chocolates and nuts. "Thank you. Yes, although the nuts would be fine, giving them all that candy right before bed wouldn't help them settle to sleep. Sugar high and all that." Noelle went over and set the bag on the kitchen table. "Okay, guys. Time to brush teeth and head to bed. Say goodnight to Turner then off with you."

She watched as Camden and Mace gave the tall lean man a hug. He'd taken his jacket off, setting it in a chair out of the way. He chatted with them for a few moments, listening carefully to what each wanted to tell him. Noelle noticed a wistful longing appear then vanish off his face. She appreciated when he waved toward the boys' bedroom, urging them to do as she'd instructed.

"You're very good with them. Thank you for not purchasing something expensive. You didn't need to bring us anything."

"Need had nothing to do with it. I wanted to. I knew you wouldn't want me to give them something out of sight price-wise. There's a saying Mamie taught me. She was my nanny, and more of a parent than mine were. 'Just because you can doesn't mean you should.' It's stood me well in many cases."

Noelle thought about that. It was a wise saying and true. Maybe it was something she needed to learn. "I need to get them into bed. Will you be all right while I do that?"

"Sure, go ahead."

Noelle helped the boys get ready for bed, and succumbed to their plea to say goodnight to Turner. They raced into the living room and soon came back. She listened to their prayers, prayed with each one, then kissed them as she tucked them beneath their covers.

When Noelle returned to the great room, Turner was sitting at the table studying her drawing. Her feelings of frustration returned. Putting off the return to her work, she said, "Can I get you anything? A soda or water?"

"Water's fine. I need to hydrate after so many hours on an airplane. What's this you're working on?"

"The sets for the Christmas play. I'm in charge of the sets and props. I'm dividing them up between various team members. Each couple of people will have one set to paint and props to get. I'm dividing up the list now. Not that I won't end up doing it all." She mumbled the last as she took two bottles of water out of the fridge.

"Why will you be doing it all?"

Noelle jumped. She didn't know he'd come up behind her. She closed the refrigerator door and leaned against it, handing him a bottle. "I always seem to end up doing everything for whatever project. Remember how many people were helping set up the Harvest Hop?"

"Just one. You."

"That's how it is most times. If the team members show up for meetings, they seem enthusiastic and have good ideas. We'll make plans and set deadlines and such. Then nothing gets done unless I do it."

"Do you accept ideas from your team, or are all of them yours?" Turner cracked open his water bottle.

"I want their ideas. Often I don't have a clue where to start on some things. For this play, it's pretty easy. There are suggested set drawings we can use. They need to be transferred to the backdrops and painted. There's a list of props for each scene.

"My plan is to divide them up amongst the team members so the load isn't all on a few people. Trouble is, I'm the only one who will actually do the painting. Some will gather a few of the props, but if they have difficulty finding something, they won't follow through or let anyone else know. Then I'll be scrambling at the last minute, trying to find or create or buy whatever is needed."

"What would happen if you just did your assigned part? If you didn't do all the rest of what's needed?"

Noelle thought about it for a moment. "Dress rehearsal would come, and the sets and props wouldn't be ready."

"And?"

"What do you mean, and?"

"What would happen then?"

"Well, I suppose the players wouldn't have what they needed to perform."

"And?"

"And I'd feel really guilty for letting everyone down."

"But you didn't. They did. You'd have your set all done, and the props you're responsible for there and ready to go."

"But I'm the team leader. Ultimately, it's my responsibility."

"So you let all the other team members shirk their duty, and take up the burden of it all. What do they learn by that?"

"What do you mean?"

"Do you want them to always think they don't have do what they've agreed to? That what they've promised to do, they can just not complete? How is that helping anyone? I know it's not your job to help people become better, more responsible adults, but it's also not your job to enable them to be irresponsible."

"Is that what I'm doing?"

"Possibly."

Noelle thought about what he was saying. Her doing what her team was supposed to do really did enable them to be irresponsible. To not fulfill their commitment to her, the team, the church, and ultimately to God.

Do all things as if you were doing them for Christ. That was something she tried to do. Do for others the way you want them to do for you. Huh, her team members weren't helping how she wanted to be helped.

Noelle looked up at Turner.

"Just because you can doesn't mean you should," he said.

"So, how do I proceed with this and not get into big trouble with my brother, who as you know is the head pastor of the church?" Noelle pursed her lips and looked at him.

Turner chuckled. "Does make it just a bit more difficult. Here's what I'd do. I'd send out an email to everyone on the team, and to Hutch, with all the information they need: your lists, places they can work on the sets, the supplies you will have ready and waiting for them to use. Everything you can think of to make it easy for them to do their part of the project.

"Set up a deadline schedule, and put that in too. Then send out reminder emails before each deadline. Be sure to send them to your brother. That way there's an e-paper trail if someone says you didn't send them a reminder. Do your assigned tasks so they are finished by the deadline. Send out an email indicating that you're done. If you want, you can say you are willing to help others. They can contact you with the time when they are going to be working. Shows your support without letting them off the hook."

"I get it. Lead by enabling their success. Give them the tools they need to complete the task."

"Then it's up to them to do it or not. If they don't, well, you've done all you can to help them. The failure will be on them if they don't."

"What if they don't, and we get to dress rehearsal and there aren't any sets?"

"Hey, yours will be there, ready and waiting. That theirs aren't..." Turner shrugged his shoulders.

"I could take a picture of mine when I get it done, and send to them."

"Good idea. Maybe some of all the props you gather, too."

"Dress rehearsal, at least the first one, is a week before the play, so we'd be able to get the sets made in time for the performance."

Turner laughed. "Yeah, it'll be a tough thing for your team members, who don't have it all done, to have everyone know they didn't. Might embarrass them enough to get their tasks done in future projects."

"Or they'll quit the team."

"Then they are dead weight anyway, and you'll be better off without them."

Heaviness lifted from Noelle's shoulders. It was a good plan. She could even think of the verses in the Bible that supported what Turner was talking about.

"Oh," Turner said. "One more thing. It won't be you getting your set painted. It will be we. I'm going to help you."

Noelle stepped away from the refrigerator and leaned against him. He wrapped his arms around her, holding her close. "Thank you. I was so stressed when you got here. Now I've got a plan as to how to proceed."

Turner set his chin on top of her head. She felt supported and protected in a way she never had before.

~~~~~

"Hey," Noelle said as she batted Turner's arm.

"What?" They were sitting at the kitchen table going over the drawings and lists, getting things organized for Noelle to send out her email to the team.

"You gave my kids those fake mice, just so they could scare me with them."

Turner started laughing. He couldn't help it. Each time she'd found one, he'd gotten a photo of it meeting its demise. They had been the highlights of his trip. He'd respond with how sorry he was for the poor mouse. There must be one more she hadn't found.

Noelle batted his shoulder again. "How many of those things did you give them, anyway."

Turner shrugged. "You know how mice multiply. There could be hundreds in here by now."

"There better not be."

He struggled to keep an evil grin off his face. He leaned over and kissed her nose. "Don't worry. They don't bite or crawl up your pant legs."

~~~~~

Lying on his stomach on the floor of the playroom, Turner was building something with Mace from the LEGO blocks. He didn't have a clue as to what it was, but Mace seemed to know and that was enough. Camden was still finishing his homework. It was Wednesday. Brad would be coming soon to pick up his sons to keep them overnight. He'd take them to school in the morning.

"Can you find me another wheel?" Mace glanced at Turner, then turned his focus back to whatever it was he was building.

"Sure." Turner started digging through the pile of pieces on the large round sheet. It was a recent addition. It had a drawstring so the pieces could be put on top and the string pulled, enclosing everything in. It enabled quick clean up. Turner had found it online and had it sent to Mr. Camden Copeland and Mr. Mace Copeland. They'd been thrilled at getting a package.

Noelle stuck her head in the room. "You need to pick up now. Your dad will be here shortly."

"Ah, Mommy, do I have to go? All Dad wants to do is sit and talk with Kimberly."

"Yes, you do, and don't complain to him about it. Do you want to take something with you to play with? You can take your backpack."

Camden squeezed past his mother, and the boys picked out some toys, putting them in a backpack. Turner noticed they each took the tops he gave them.

The doorbell rang, and Noelle went to answer it.

"Did you put more mice in the marker bag?" Camden asked in a loud whisper.

Turner grinned and nodded as he stood up. The smiles on two small faces grew wide.

"Mommy still hasn't found the one in her snow boot," Mace said.

"It can stay there until it snows and she needs to wear it. Now, shush about them or she'll hear." Turner ruffled Camden's hair.

Brad Copeland came into the room. "Ready boys?" Then he noticed Turner. "Evening."

"Brad."

There was an awkward silence. Or at least Turner thought Brad looked uncomfortable. Maybe it was because he'd called the man by his name, even though Brad hadn't returned the courtesy.

"Well, come on guys. Kim is waiting in the car." Brad

picked up a gym bag that held clothing for tomorrow. Camden slung the backpack onto his shoulder. Both boys looked at Turner.

"Bye, Turner. See you later. Thanks for playing Legos with me." Mace fist-bumped him and ran to get his coat.

Camden glanced at the marker bag and grinned. "Come on, Dad. Let's go."

It wasn't long before only he and Noelle were alone in the house. Turner wandered from the playroom and found her standing in the great room. The pensive look on her face made him move to her and pull her into an embrace.

"What's the matter?"

"This is the first time Mace has said he doesn't want to go to his dad's. Camden didn't want to go either. They're only four and six, and don't want to go to there for the night. Kim is always there, and makes it pretty clear she doesn't want them around. I don't think they ever get a home cooked meal either. They have take out. Last week they had what Camden and Mace called 'stinky food.' I think it was Indian, but I'm not sure.

"They've set up a playroom with a TV and game console. That's where the boys are supposed to stay until bedtime. Then they eat a bowl of cereal before going to bed. They never have anything good like ice cream. Kim doesn't do dairy."

"Not really child friendly."

"No, Camden said he nearly starved last weekend. They had some vegan stuff to eat. Tufu, he called it, with broccoli, weird colored olives that tasted awful, Brussel sprouts and leeks. Mace couldn't figure out what was leaking. They both said they nearly starved.

'Mom, why can't we just have real food like corn dogs and French fries?'" Noelle raised her voice, sounding like a child.

"I know what they mean. I was raised eating what Kyria and I called 'grown up food,' when we ate with our parents. Usually, we left the table hungry. Then we'd go find Mamie. She'd have real food for us." Turner made air quotes.

Noelle ran her hand through her hair. "The next night they had pizza with spinach, artichokes, and vegan cheese."

Turner groaned then laughed. "I have a pretty sophisticated palate, and I wouldn't do spinach, artichoke, vegan cheese pizza. Sounds gross. What do you suppose they'll have for supper tonight?"

"Brad told me they'd picked up Chinese. At least the boys will eat fried rice, and they get the sweet and sour chicken without the sauce. It's like chicken nuggets."

"Maybe they won't starve then."

"I just worry Camden will start refusing to go. He may only be six, but he's stubborn." Noelle looked at him. He saw an anger there he hadn't before. "I'm trying to keep my cool about Brad, but it's getting harder. He's their dad. They're supposed to be important to him. He should be more involved in their lives, especially when they are with him. Instead, he's focused on Kim.

"I get that I wasn't what he wanted. I'm coming to understand that it's not something lacking in me. It's hard, but I'm learning." She gave a sad chuckle. "He's making that easier with how he's acting. It's how he's treating the boys.

"They used to look forward to him picking them up.

Now they don't want to go. Turner, they are only four and six. They don't understand why their dad doesn't want to do anything with them.

"Now, I have to balance my anger toward Brad, not showing it to the boys, as well as not saying things against him, and Mace and Camden not wanting to go stay with him. I feel like I'm stuck between a rock and a hard place, with no one to help me get unstuck."

She looked so forlorn. Turner couldn't think of anything to say that might help either how she felt, or how to help fix the problem. Instead, he just gathered her in his arms and held her. He knew it was the right thing when she relaxed against him, slipping her arms around his back and holding on to him.

CHAPTER SEVEN

Noelle stepped back and looked at the flat she'd just covered in white primer. Sure some of the previous layer of paint showed through, but that would be covered with the design for this play. Saturday, she planned to draw out the design and begin painting.

She and Turner had gone to The Fortified Burger for supper, and pigged out on their fresh French fries. He'd never been there before, so she had to explain that most of the condiments you wanted were mixed in with the ground meat before it was flame grilled. Turner had pronounced it 'real food,' making her laugh.

Then they'd gone shopping for the supplies needed to create the sets for the Christmas play. Noelle had to explain that they were on a budget and couldn't purchase every color of paint, when Turner had started loading up the cart.

"Not a problem," he said. "I'll buy it. If it's not used for this production, I'm sure it will be used some other time. Are you sure that's enough primer? I don't want the team to run out, and not get their set made because they ran out."

"I think three gallons will be plenty. I don't think we used one to cover the flats the last time we painted them." Noelle put one gallon back on the shelf.

"Oh, this is a great color. Let's get a gallon of this." Turner lifted a gallon of neon green. It was the same color as his folding bicycle.

"I think a quart will be enough. I'm not sure when it will be used. Most likely not for this production. Maybe for vacation Bible school. The kids would love it."

Noelle laughed to herself as Turner picked up neon pink, orange, and yellow, along with the bright green. He seemed to be enjoying the thought of painting the flats.

"Have you ever done anything like this before, Turner?"

"Not really. Maybe I did some in college, I can't remember. Those years are sort of a blur. I was taking far more than a full load of classes, and attending functions in England and around Europe for my parents. It saved them from having to travel to the continent as often."

"Kyria has told me a little about how sheltered she was while growing up. Were you as restricted as she was?" Noelle wished she hadn't asked the question when Turner's expression changed from boyish delight to solemn and guarded.

"I was the reason she was so stifled. Well, not really me, but what happened to me." Turner set the cans of paint in the cart. "When I was eleven, I was kidnapped. I think they wanted to hold me for ransom. They'd tied me up in the basement of where they were hiding out and left me there. I was able to cut the ropes on a sharp piece of metal sticking out of the wall. Then, I broke out one of the windows and, being as skinny as I was, climbed out. I ran for several blocks, then found a convenience store. I went in and told the clerk what had happened. She called the police and my family.

"Bodyguards were the result. I was at least a bit older than Kyria. She wasn't quite five at the time. She never really had a chance to be anything but, as she calls it, wrapped in bubble wrap."

"Wow, how terrifying."

"Yeah, I was pretty scared. They told me they'd been following me for several weeks. That scared the… Well, you get the idea. That's when I began studying martial arts. I wanted to be able to defend myself if anyone ever tried to kidnap or attack me again."

"You any good at it?" Noelle looked at his slim, muscular body. He had on his ever-present leather jacket.

"You name the style and it's probable I have a black belt in it. Some are several degree belts." He struck a wide-legged pose, holding his hands up. "These hands are lethal weapons. They are registered with the FBI." He made chopping motions and knocked several paint brushes from a hook.

"Put those away. Nothing needs murdering here."

"Yes, ma'am." Turner stuck his hands in his jacket pockets.

~~~~~

"Don't you have anything, um, older, more, I don't know, rattier to wear? You're going to get paint on them. They'll be ruined for anything other than this sort of stuff, cleaning, and yard work."

Turner looked at what Noelle was wearing, then

down at himself. She had on sweats that were frayed and covered with paint spots and other unidentifiable stains. Her sneakers, that may have been white at one time, were worn, with spots matching those on her clothes.

"Um, no. I bought these at Wally World. I don't think I've ever worn anything as inexpensive as these. I don't care if I get paint on them or the shoes. Bought them there too. I'm surprised at how comfortable they are." He lifted one foot and circled his ankle, showing off the navy deck shoe he was wearing.

Noelle just shook her head at him. "Let's go. We've got a lot to get done today." She shrugged her pea coat on and took her purse off a hook in the closet. When she reached for several grocery sacks full of things, Turner grabbed them and winked at her.

"I'll carry these for you." He bowed and swept the bags toward the door. "After you."

Turner opened the passenger door of his SUV for her, then put the bags in the back seat. Once he was buckled in, he started the car and pulled out of her driveway.

Noelle sighed. "Camden protested going to Brad's this morning. I was able to talk him into not complaining to his dad, at least for now. I'm not sure how much longer I can keep him from it."

"I thought they were to be picked up last night."

"That's the agreement. Every Wednesday and every other Friday to Sunday. Brad called yesterday and said he and Kim were going out last night, and he couldn't take the boys until this morning. Some concert of a band I've never heard of. Made me feel really old."

Turner chuckled. "I know what you mean. The

popular music I hear on the radio, I have no clue who the bands are."

"Brad gets them for Thanksgiving this year. It's spelled out per year in the custody agreement, that whoever has them for Thanksgiving doesn't have them for Christmas. Each year is listed with who has who. If one of us can't have them that day, it's forfeited. Stops any manipulations."

Turner glanced over at Noelle. That she was a bit depressed was obvious. He couldn't think of what to say to make her feel better. The situation between her sons and their father had to be difficult. She understood how her boys felt, but was powerless to help them make it better. The courts mandated that they had to be with him on the specified days. Only if Brad didn't want them could they skip being with him.

Turner pulled into the church parking lot. Several cars were there. "I'm surprised there're any other people here."

"Why? Generally, there's something going on. I think there's a men's prayer breakfast. I know they are having rehearsal for the play. Camden's class is singing in act two, but they don't need to be at all the practices. Can you imagine twelve six-year-olds at every practice, waiting around to sing one song?" She laughed. "Not a good idea."

Turner followed her down the stairs into the basement. There was a large unfinished room where they'd be painting the flats. Each group on the team had flats or sets to paint or build. Since Noelle didn't know anything about construction, she was in charge of painting two flats.

"Usually Whitney builds the most difficult sets, but

with her laid up, I've had to spread what she normally does between several other groups." Noelle set the bags of supplies on a table near the wall. There were saw horses as well as several old, beat-up tables scattered around the room. The walls were cinder block. Fluorescent lights hung from the floor joists above them.

Listening to her explain how to enlarge and draw the outline of the various parts of the design, Turner drew the grids on the flat, then began on the other while Noelle sketched the outlines. He'd finished the second flat when they heard footsteps descending the stairs. He moved over to where they'd laid their jackets on a table, leaning casually against it, his arms crossed over his chest. From that position, he could move quickly in any direction.

Hutch came in carrying what looked to be a large rock. Following was Liam, the leader of the adult Sunday school class, and a teenage boy. They, too, carried rocks.

"Hey, Noelle, Turner," Hutch greeted them. "Liam and Kyle brought the rocks they made at home. Aren't they great?" He made motions as if he was going to throw the rock at him. It was one of the stage props Turner knew had been assigned to be made.

Noelle laid her pencil on the flat. "Wonderful. How about you set them over there." She pointed to a corner where they would be out of the way. "They look great. So real. Thank you for getting them done so quickly. I really appreciate it.

After they'd relieved themselves of their burdens, Liam said, "You emailing the assignments, and what supplies were available, and where they were really helped. I had all the information on my phone. Then Kyle looked up how to make the rocks online. We were able to do them in the garage. Made it easy to get them done."

Kyle had run out and up the steps, after he'd set his rock down. Now he was back with another one, as well as a tote bag of supplies. "We took these home with us. Where do you want them?" When he'd put the rock with the others, and helped Turner sort the contents of the tote, Kyle asked, "Want some help with the painting? I can stay and help, can't I, Dad?"

"Sure," both Noelle and Liam said at the same time.

"We can bring him home," Turner added. "I'll even treat him to lunch. A thank you for helping."

Hutch went up to his office, and Liam left. Noelle, Turner, and Kyle began painting. Noelle had laid it out like a paint by number, making it easy to know where to paint what color. Kyle quickly showed talent as an artist, adding shading and texture Noelle was planning to add later after the paint dried.

"Your ability is going to save me a lot of time and effort. It's going to be much better also. So much more realistic."

"Thanks. I like art. Since I can't go out for sports, I can work on art projects at home."

"Why can't you go out for sports?" Turner knew it might be impolite to ask, but the young man seemed pretty open about it.

"I have to watch my brothers and sisters after school until Dad gets home. Mom died three years ago." Kyle's hand holding the paint brush stilled.

Turner placed a hand on his shoulder. "I'm real sorry for your loss. I was older, an adult, when my parents died, but it was still tough."

"Your folks both died?"

"Yes, they were killed in an airplane crash. All of a sudden they were just gone." Turner didn't mention that he hadn't been very close to them. Kyle needed to know someone knew what it was like to lose a parent. "It's tough."

"Yeah, it is."

They continued painting, then Noelle stated she needed to head to the ladies room. Once she was out of hearing range Turner grinned and tapped Kyle on the shoulder.

"You want to do something for me?"

"What?"

"Paint a mouse right there." He pointed to a spot on the flat. "It doesn't have to be very big. No one in the audience even needs to be able to see it."

"Why?"

Turner had moved to the doorway. He glanced out and came back across to where Kyle was standing. "Noelle's afraid of mice. Her boys and I have been hiding toy mice all over her house as a joke."

Kyle laughed. "I get it. Sure. Get me the gray paint."

Turner brought the can over and, in a shorter time than he could have imagined, a small mouse peeked out from a doorway on the flat. He'd been keeping a lookout for Noelle, and was getting concerned when she came down the stairs.

"Sorry it took me so long. Chloe and Noah stopped in to talk with Hutch. I met her in the hall. She and the baby are going shopping. Hutch asked if he could join us for lunch. I said it was okay."

"Fine with me. Come on. Let's get some more work

done. You've been slacking, woman. Wasting all that time playing with a baby." Turner leaned over, put his shoulder in her stomach and hefted her over his shoulder. She squawked, and smacked him on the back as he carried her across the room. Setting her on her feet where she'd been working before, he pointed at the flat and said, "Paint."

"Yes, sir." Noelle saluted and Kyle, standing nearby with a paintbrush in his hand, laughed.

~~~~~

"What are your intentions toward my sister?"

Turner glanced over at Hutch, seated in the passenger seat of the Macan. They were heading to get sandwiches to bring back to the church for themselves, Noelle, and Kyle.

He thought about the question. He understood Hutch's concerns. He'd had the same concerns when he'd found out Kyria was engaged. They weren't identical, but he was the older brother and did love his sister, even though he'd not been present in her life for several years. Although it hadn't been his intention, Kyria had felt abandoned by him.

Turner's life had taken a sharp left turn with their parents' deaths. He'd traveled the world several times over, not keeping in good contact with Kyria or the lawyer who handled their trusts and businesses.

That he couldn't explain his actions bothered Turner. Soon though, one way or the other, everything would come to its conclusion. Until then, not only couldn't he reveal anything, but he also couldn't or shouldn't make plans for the future.

"I'm really attracted to Noelle, Hutch. I like the boys. She's a wonderful mother, and I love being with her.

We have fun together. I enjoy playing with Camden and Mace, too."

"They aren't toys, Turner. Not something you can take out when you want to, and then put back on the shelf when you don't want to play. They've had enough of that from their dad."

"I know. All I really know at this point is that I'll not do anything to hurt Noelle or the boys. There's a project I'm working on that was supposed to come to a close sometime early next year. Instead, the timetable has been moved up.

"As much as I hate it, I'll be going on several more overseas trips over the next few weeks. If all goes well, the project may be complete by Christmas. If not, then not too long after."

"Thanks for the explanation, but it doesn't answer my question." Hutch turned slightly in his seat so he could look at Turner.

"It's really too soon to tell if what seems to be developing between us has any sort of future. This project needs to complete before I can make any plans. Until we know the results of it— well, I just can't commit to anything else. With that said, my intentions are honorable. You don't need to worry on that score."

"Good, Noelle's been through enough. Camden and Mace, too. I don't want her, or them, disappointed and hurt because you simply leave after the holidays."

"If all goes as planned, I'm thinking of buying a house or condo here in town. I'm hoping to settle in one place. My entire life has been spent traveling from one place to another. I've never really had anywhere I considered home." Turner sighed. "Home was pretty much wherever Mamie was. Kyria's going to be here, and I want to be close to her. She's the only family I have. Once the project is complete, I should be able to do that. At least I hope so."

Turner stopped before he revealed something he shouldn't. He hoped everything worked out so Kyria would be safe, and he could simply stay in one place and set down roots. His family had traveled so much while he was growing up. Once he was out of university, Turner had taken over small amounts of the businesses the family owned. He was being groomed for eventually taking over control.

When his and Kyria's parents were killed in the plane crash, Russ Naylor, the family's lawyer, had assumed most of the responsibility for the businesses. Turner had rebelled and gone off adventure seeking as a way to deal with his loss. In the process, he'd pretty much abandoned Kyria.

Then he'd been contacted about the circumstances of the jet's crash, and nothing had been the same since. Turner thought he'd found the ultimate adventure. Now, it was a pressing burden he carried, and would until all his tasks were complete and the goal accomplished. He only hoped he'd be able to make plans for his future after that.

The expression on Hutch's face indicated that he wasn't totally pleased with Turner's answer. There wasn't anything more he could say to reassure Noelle's brother.

CHAPTER EIGHT

Noelle picked up her phone. It was ringing with the tone she had programmed in for Brad. She thought to put it on speaker so she could continue to work on the corn casserole she was preparing for Thanksgiving dinner tomorrow, but decided not to. He was supposed to be picking the boys up shortly so they could spend Thanksgiving with him. Him calling this close to when he was supposed to pick them up didn't bode well for that.

She'd be spending the day at the Jenner family home with Hutch, Chloe, and baby Noah. Noelle's and Hutch's parents were out of town as this was the year they spent the holiday with their sister in Utah. They wouldn't be here for Christmas either since they were living in Arizona for the winter, near their brother. Both holidays had been celebrated with them in late October before they left for the warmer climate of the southwest.

"Hello?" Noelle said.

"Noelle, um, I need to make a change of plans."

"Oh?"

Brad cleared his throat. "Yeah, I can't have the boys

tomorrow. Kim and I are going out of town to her folks. We're staying overnight there and, um, aren't coming back until Sunday. I got off work for Friday."

Noelle gritted her teeth, counted to ten before saying, "Okay, that's not a problem. Just remember one thing, Brad. You know that in the custody agreement it says, if you give up your rights on a holiday, you don't get them for a different one. You forfeit your rights to them. In other words, you won't have them Christmas just because you didn't have them for Thanksgiving."

"Yeah, I know. No problem. Thanks for understanding. Talk to you later. Gotta go. Have a happy Thanksgiving. Bye."

Noelle's phone screen read: 'Call Ended.' She bit back a curse. Saying a swear word wouldn't help the situation. She stood considering for a moment, thinking about Brad and his behavior toward his sons.

Granted, this wasn't his weekend to have the boys. He'd just had them last weekend. They had traded weekends in the past. Here he could have had them for four nights and four days. Spent some real quality time with them. Brad had taken Friday off work.

That stuck in Noelle's craw. He'd never done that for her. Never once had he taken an extra day off work to spend time with her and the boys. Kim, well, that seemed to be a different story.

Noelle thought about the increasing number of times Brad hadn't taken the boys on his scheduled days. Several times recently, she'd suggested they switch weekends. Only once had he taken her up on it. The rest he just skipped his opportunity to be with his sons.

She went down the hall to the playroom. Camden and Mace were playing while they waited for their father to pick them up. As she stood in the doorway, Noelle wondered whether they would be disappointed they weren't spending Thanksgiving with their dad. Unfortunately, she didn't think so.

It made her so angry that he was shirking his duty to them. That he was more interested in Kim than his flesh and blood. She thought about Mark's slip of the tongue and grinned a bit snarkily. Yes, she was a bimbo.

Well, Noelle loved her boys, and was delighted for herself that she got to have them for Thanksgiving. They would have fun at the Jenners. Hutch and Chloe's son, Noah, was eleven-months-old now and loved having his cousins come and play. Chloe was a Jenner. She and Noelle had been best friends growing up.

"Hey, guys." Noelle stepped into the room. Two sets of eyes looked up at her. "There's been a complication. You're not going to your dad's for Thanksgiving. You'll be coming with me to the Jenners'."

"Is anything wrong?" Camden asked.

"No, just a change of plans. Is that okay with you?"

"Yep," Mace said.

"Sure. I wasn't wanting to be with Kim anyway. She just complains we make too much noise." Camden's focus went back to the action figures scattered around on the floor.

Noelle started to leave them to their play, then turned back around. "Do you guys have a notebook you could give me? I need one."

"Sure, Mommy." Mace jumped up and got one from a shelf. "I think there's only a couple of pages with stuff on them. You can keep it. We have more."

Noelle took it and leaned down, kissing his head. "Thanks. I'll let you know when supper's ready. It may be a while. I hadn't planned on you two eating with me."

They assured her they could wait, after finding out that ice cream and chips weren't what she had in mind for their meal.

Before Noelle began fixing supper, she listed all the times in the last few months that Brad hadn't taken the boys on his appointed days in the notebook she'd gotten from his sons.

~~~~~

The ringing of his cell phone pulled Turner out of a sound sleep. The specific ringtone brought him totally awake. He picked it up, swiping to connect the call. The clock on the bedside table read 2:37.

"Yes," he growled into the phone.

"I need you in Morocco by Monday. I'll send the details. Our contact has set up a meeting. It's vital you're there."

"Fine, but I'll make my own travel arrangements. Also, I want to be supplied with weapons, as well as the other equipment I need to get this done. I can't take those through security."

"Your driver will have everything you need. We've booked your hotel reservations." There was a chuckle. "I'll let you book your flights. Just be sure to be there by Monday in enough time to be at the meeting."

Turner didn't respond. He just ended the call. They both knew he'd be there.

He lay in bed looking up into the darkness. Things were coming to a head. It was only about two weeks ago that he'd gone to Monte Carlo and Tel Aviv. Now, he was headed to Morocco. Just a bit too close, both in time and distance.

A shudder ran through his body. He'd been under surveillance on his last trip. He knew it. He'd felt the eyes watching his every move. Felt the vulnerability of being weaponless. Felt the weight of his assigned tasks.

Well, he wouldn't sleep for a while. Might as well book his flights. He'd need to leave sometime on Sunday to make it to Morocco on time.

Turner flipped on the light and pulled his laptop over. Soon, he had an open-ended reservation, which allowed him to go to church with Noelle and the boys, before leaving for the airport. It would be tight, but he didn't want to miss the opportunity to be with her.

~~~~~

Turner pulled the Macan into Noelle's driveway and put the car in park. He was picking her up before they went to the Jenner family home. Mark's parents often hosted large family gatherings. Noelle, being a life-long friend of their daughter Chloe, was always welcome.

When Mark's mother, Heather, found out Noelle would be alone on Thanksgiving, she'd insisted she spend the day with them. An invitation for Turner to join the celebration had been extended as soon as she knew he would be in town for the holiday. He'd been invited for Christmas as well.

There were several bottles of wine in the back he would take in as hostess gifts. Mark had assured him that they would be most welcome.

Turner checked his pockets as he walked to her front door. Before he pressed the doorbell, the door opened and Mace stood there, smiling up at him.

"Hi, Turner. Dad cancelled. We get to go and play

with all the kids at Jenners'."

"That'll be fun." Turner wondered what caused the change of plans. He followed as Mace ran into the great room.

"Turner's here, Mommy," the boy yelled.

Camden was sitting on the floor playing a video game. "Hey, Turner."

"Hi, Camden. Happy Thanksgiving."

"Yeah, happy turkey day." He giggled at his joke.

Turner moved into the kitchen where Noelle was taking a casserole out of the oven. Once she placed it on the counter, Turner pulled her to him, hugging her against his chest. "Why'd Brad cancel?" He kissed her ear as he whispered the question.

"They decided to go to her parents' for the weekend and didn't want the boys." Bitterness laced her words.

Turner couldn't understand why a father wouldn't want to be with his children for a holiday. He knew how it felt to be alone on special days. His parents had missed many of his and Kyria's birthdays, as well as holidays. It was something he'd never do to any children he ever had. Or Noelle's, for that matter, if their relationship progressed.

"I'd say I'm sorry, but I'm glad they will be with us," Turner said. "I'd have missed them today."

Noelle lifted watery eyes to look at him, searching his face. What she saw must have reassured her that his words were true. "Thank you. I was pretty angry when Brad called. Then I realized I would have them and decided to count my blessings."

"But you still are hurt that Brad ditched them."

She laid her head on his chest. "Yes, I am. Children grow so fast. These are his children. Shouldn't he want to be with them on holidays?"

"Were they upset about not going with him?" Turner rubbed his hand up and down her back.

"No, and that's sad in itself."

"You get used to it after a while. Your parents not being there for things. I was angry about it for a long time."

"Your parents missed a lot of events?"

Turner set his chin on her head. "Holidays, birthdays, that sort of thing. We were homeschooled, so no events like those. Even though we often traveled with them, we didn't see them much. We were with Mamie and whatever tutor we had at the time."

"Sounds sad. And lonely."

"I suppose it was. It was all I ever knew so it was normal for me. For us, Kyria and me. She's so much younger that I was used to being alone by the time she was born."

Noelle stepped back, out of his arms. "I need to get the food ready to go." She took a roll of aluminum foil out of a drawer and pulled off a strip. "She's around seven years younger, right?"

"Yes. I think that year we spent Easter in Connecticut. Mom was expecting her real soon, and they wanted her to be born in the States. It was the only time I remember going to worship service with them."

Noelle finished covering the casserole and leaned against the counter. "Are all disgustingly wealthy parents as distant as yours were?"

Turner laughed. "I can't say for all, but some. There were a few times when they would take us with them to visit other disgustingly wealthy families. It seemed that many were similar to ours." Turner thought for a moment. "Maybe not all as paranoid about kidnapping or other threats as mine, but still rather distant. We kids would often be left with the nannies or tutors while the parents entertained themselves elsewhere. Don't get me wrong. There was lots to entertain us. Toys, video games, movies, swimming pools, ski lifts, four-wheelers. You name something money can buy and we had it."

Noelle got a carrier out and put the casserole into it. "Hey, guys. Time to get ready to go," she called. They spent the next few minutes finding shoes, filling a backpack with favorite toys, and putting on coats.

"Here," Turner said. "You go get yourself ready and I'll take this and the boys out to the car. We'll move the car seats over."

Noelle smiled and gave him a quick kiss as she passed by, heading to her bedroom. "Thanks. I'll hurry."

When she was out of earshot, Turner bent down and looked at the two boys who had come to mean a great deal to him. He pulled three furry gray mice out of his jacket pocket.

"I'll put this one in the casserole carrier. You guys find someplace to put these. Don't you think it would be fun to scare your mom some today?"

Mace covered his mouth with his hands, stifling his giggles, and nodded. "I know where to put one. Mommy always takes her crocheting when we spend the day at the Jenners. I'll stick mine in there."

"Good idea, Mace. Do you have an idea, Camden?"

He nodded. "I'll save mine for later. I can stick it in her shoe. We always take them off when we get there.

That way she'll find it just before we come home."

Turner laughed. "Another good idea." He tucked the toy mouse onto the top of the foil covered dish, and zipped the carrier closed. "Come on. Let's get our stuff done so we're ready when she comes out."

~~~~~

Noelle unzipped the carrier to remove her corn casserole and grinned. "Eeeek," she screamed out the doorway of the kitchen. Giggles and hands slapping together were heard coming from the family room.

"What's that about?" Chloe asked, returning from the dining room after delivering a bowl of salad.

"It's a bit of a story."

"Well, spill, girl." It was Rachel Jenner, wife of the oldest son, Luke, who commanded.

Noelle laughed. "It started the night before the Harvest Hop. I was setting up, and a mouse ran across the floor. It startled me and Turner came running in. I had to confess it was a mouse. He's teased me ever since and enlisted the boys, too. They hide these toy mice all over the place. They startled me at first. Now I just scream 'eek' and go on. They get a kick out of it." She held up the small toy for all the women in the kitchen to see.

Chloe took it from her. "You've always been afraid of mice. Very afraid. I think you're downplaying this."

Noelle felt her cheeks flame.

"Now, I know you are. Come on. We need the details."

"I know the whole story. Turner told me," Kyria said. She was putting yeast rolls in a basket. "Noelle was standing on a table when he got in the building. She said the mouse was this big." She held her arms wide.

The roll she was holding was plucked from her hand.

"That she was," Turner said from behind Kyria. He moved nearer to Noelle and wrapped an arm around her waist. "She was jumping around on the table, messing up the tablecloth. I had to use my Velcro leg guards on her ankles before she'd get down off the table. She was scared a mouse would crawl up her pant leg." He took a bite out of the roll. "Wow, these are wonderful rolls."

"Mother Lee's rolls. Best there ever was. Old family recipe." This was said by Trina Jenner, Gavin's wife.

Noelle was thoroughly embarrassed now. She didn't think she'd ever live down her escapade with the mouse at the Harvest Hop. Especially since all the Jenners were going to know about it. All the wives would share the story with their husbands.

Noelle glanced at Chloe, whose eyes were shining with mischief. Great, now Hutch would tease her unmercifully. She'd kept mum about it just so she wouldn't have to endure the teasing. Her brother was a wicked tease even though he was a minister. Surely there was a Bible verse that forbade that. She'd have to look.

CHAPTER NINE

Camden and Mace were wound up and bouncy as Noelle tried to get them ready for bed. While she was helping Camden put his pajamas on, Mace ran naked out of the bedroom to tell Turner something. Fortunately, he was sent right back in to put some clothes on that bare bottom. While she corralled Mace into his PJs, Camden jumped on his bed, slipped, and fell off, leading to howls and tears. He wasn't hurt, which Noelle was thankful for, but her patience was wearing thin.

A loud clearing of a throat had all three people in the room looking toward the door. Turner stood there with a frown on his face.

"Seems to me there are a couple of boys who aren't being obedient or respectful to their mother. It's been a long day, and I'm sure she's tired. How about you guys be considerate to her by going to bed properly like I know you can?" He raised an eyebrow and jerked his head toward one bed then the other.

Camden and Mace looked at each other, at Noelle, then back at him. Mace hugged her. "Sorry, Mommy."

Camden did the same. "I'm sorry too. I know I'm not

supposed to jump on the bed."

"Thank you. Now, let's go brush teeth."

"Can Turner come too?" Mace asked, gazing up at the tall good-looking man.

Inwardly, Noelle sighed. Both boys were beginning to have a bit of hero worship toward Turner. He paid attention to them, listened and played with them. He was filling a need that was supposed to be filled by their father. It concerned her. What if he left, going back to his high society life and didn't keep in contact? How would that affect Camden and Mace?

Turner was only here for the holidays. At least that's what the plan had been when Kyria had told Noelle about her brother coming to town and staying with her. One holiday was now history. Christmas was about a month away. Then a week later would be New Years. After that— who knew what Turner would do.

He'd mentioned possibly finding his own place, but Noelle hadn't seen any evidence of him doing so. She also wondered whether he'd be satisfied actually living in one place, rather than jetting all over the world on a moment's notice. She was sure he owned multiple properties in more desirable locations than Benton. Kyria had mentioned one in the Caribbean somewhere and another in Italy or Switzerland, she couldn't remember. Kyria mentioned living in so many countries growing up it got confusing.

All Noelle really knew was that her sons would be devastated if he left and never contacted them again. She would be too.

She'd let Turner supervise the teeth brushing while she picked up the discarded clothing. Running footsteps of two boys was heard before they flew into the room and jumped on their beds, diving under the covers.

"Hey, guys," Turner said. "You promised you'd settle down and go to sleep. I don't think running down the hall demonstrates that."

"Sorry," two not very repentant voices said.

"Well, say your prayers and go to sleep. I'll see you next time."

Noelle watched as Turner tucked the blankets around the shoulders of each boy and ruffled his hair a bit. She was glad he didn't give them a kiss. That amount of affection needed more of a commitment from him than there was at this point.

Soon, the light was switched off, admonition to go to sleep given, and the door shut behind Noelle and Turner. They went to the great room. Turner flopped down on the sofa.

"Wow, are they always this wound up after a big day?"

Noelle chuckled. "Pretty much. Thanks for the help. Hearing from a man for them to be respectful of my needs was welcome. Would you like something to drink?"

"No, I'm fine." Turner reached his hand up and taking her wrist, gave a quick pull so she fell down onto the sofa beside him. Well, half lying on him. "This is what I want." He wrapped his arms around her, pulling her close. His lips came down and met hers as she raised her head to meet his halfway.

The kiss, or maybe kisses, Noelle wasn't certain, was gentle but filled with passion. His hand slipped through her hair to cradle the back of her head. He tasted wonderful, like chocolate and rainbows and wine.

When he broke the kiss, they were both breathless. Turner hugged her to him and she got the impression it was almost in desperation.

"Noelle, I..." He paused, then looked down, searching her face. "I'm so very attracted to you. Everyday when I wake up you are the first thing on my mind. Are you awake yet? Are the boys up? What are you doing right then? Have you left the house yet? Is everyone healthy and happy?

"On days I don't see you— they just aren't good days. Not that anything is a problem. They just aren't good days. Even talking with you on the phone isn't truly enough."

Turner kissed her again. Noelle thought the next words he'd say were ones she desperately wanted to hear. Noelle hadn't realized she'd fallen in love with him, but now she knew. Head over heels. Everything he'd said about thinking of her first thing in the morning echoed how she was feeling.

Turner released her lips and looked at her. The expression in his eyes dispelled the anticipation of his next words. Sorrow, regret, and worry fought for dominance.

"I have to travel again this weekend. I've booked my flight for mid-afternoon Sunday. It'll cut me close on getting to my meeting on time, but I wanted to go to church with you and the boys. I should be back by Wednesday. Can we plan to go out to supper that night?"

Noelle pulled out of his arms and moved to the other end of the sofa. "Where are you going?"

Turner looked away. "I'm not going to say. It's not because of you, that I don't trust you. This project is top secret, and the competition would love to know any detail. They know everyone involved and may even have bugs and surveillance in your house."

"What?" Noelle nearly screeched the word. "Bugs, surveillance? What sort of project is this? I thought it was some business deal."

"Corporations will resort to all sorts of espionage to get the upper hand in a deal. Don't worry. There's no danger to you or the boys. I'd never allow that."

"You better not." Noelle slumped against the arm of the sofa. "You leave Sunday and get back Wednesday. Will you be able to text or call?"

"Maybe, I'll try. I'll be in meetings much of the time." Turner rubbed his face with his hands. "We've almost got this deal complete. I'm hoping this will be the last trip, but there may be a few more. I hate it. Especially now, during the holidays. I wanted to spend a couple of months just visiting my sister. You, the boys. I never thought I'd find someone, someones, you and the boys, who would come to mean so much to me in such a short amount of time.

"Please, don't be angry or disappointed with me. I'm going to wrap this project up as quickly, and with as few more trips as I can. Maybe this will be the last. We can hope."

Noelle looked at him. Studied his face. He seemed sincere, nearly terrified that she'd kick him out of her life. She knew if she did, he'd go. He'd honor her choice. As unsure as Noelle was about their relationship and its future, she knew she wasn't going to end it now. She wanted, no needed to see if they did have any chance at a future. Another business trip shouldn't be the deciding factor.

~~~~~

Buckling his seat belt, Turner looked at Noelle's house. He knew she wasn't happy about his leaving again so soon. He wasn't either. Two weeks between trips wasn't ideal, but it couldn't be helped. Maybe this would be the last one needed. He didn't really think that would be the case, but he could hope. And pray.

Being back in church, though he hadn't planned on attending while he was in Benton no matter how often Kyria invited him to attend, had renewed something in Turner he hadn't even realized was missing. Mamie's teachings and advice came to mind as he listened in the Sunday school class and heard Hutch preach.

As a child and teen, he didn't pay much attention to the practical aspects of the Bible. Sure, he remembered the Golden Rule and not judging others, and tried to live by them. Looking into the broader picture of what living Biblically meant hadn't ever crossed his mind. Now he'd even started reading the Bible again, having downloaded it onto his phone.

As he drove across town, Turner set the project before the throne, presenting it as an offering for success, for justice to be fulfilled. He didn't know if God would bless what was going to happen or not. Turner simply prayed that his will matched up with God's. That he was working for God's plan rather than against it.

CHAPTER TEN

Turner pulled his suitcase behind him as he exited customs in Casablanca's busy airport. Spying his name on a tablet held by a driver, he approached. "Bonjour," he said. Fluent in French, Turner chose to speak that rather than his less than proficient Arabic.

Soon they were in the car headed to his hotel. Unfortunately, the driver explained, it wasn't as close to where the meeting would take place as he'd like. Also, a reception had been scheduled last minute in another part of the city. He'd been contacted that his services would not be needed to bring Turner back to his hotel. Rather than object, the driver had added several items to the case Turner would take with him when he checked in. He advised Turner to check them over carefully as some might be slightly different from what he was familiar with.

As soon as Turner was in his room, he ran the app on his phone that scanned for bugs and hidden cameras, finding none. Then he opened the case. He smiled at the Sig Sauer hand gun and Beretta Pico. The first he was sure would be confiscated when he entered the building where the meeting was to be held. The other was small enough to be missed, especially in the body conforming concealed holster he'd carry it in.

There was a lock pick set that was nearly as nice as the one he carried but had to leave in the States. The comb gave him pause for a moment. When he picked it up and examined it more closely Turner noticed a line in an unusual place. He pulled, and a ceramic knife attached to the comb's handle slipped out. It even had a finger guard. Sweet, he thought.

Glancing at the clock, Turner decided he had plenty of time for a shower. He did so and then began his preparations for the meeting.

Contact lenses which would take images when he blinked twice at a certain rhythm were inserted. Shirt button covers, one of which recorded audio, were checked. Both would record to his phone. The body concealed holster was strapped onto his inner thigh. Once he was relieved of the Sig Sauer, he'd excuse himself to the restroom and move the Pico to a more convenient location for quick access.

The lock pick set was secured in a pocket of his leather jacket under the arm along the sleeve. He checked to be sure the special micro SD card was in place in his phone. The comb he tucked into his left leg pants pocket. Several other items were stowed in various pockets all over his jacket.

There was a sturdy envelope in the case Turner hadn't looked into yet. He frowned as he fanned the hundreds of Euros he'd taken from it. He understood the need, but it still irked that people would only do what was right for money. Slipping the money back into the envelope, he tucked it into the interior breast pocket of his jacket.

Turner studied the map of Casablanca with red circles scattered across its surface. Several were labeled. Others weren't. The locations of the hotel, meeting and the reception were marked. The other circles were between the hotel and the other places. Turner figured they were places he could hide if necessary. He took a photo with his phone. If he needed to find a safe spot, Turner didn't want to have to rely on his memory of the map.

He checked that the phone number the driver had given him was plugged in. If he needed extraction from a hideout that was the number he'd call.

His phone chirped. The driver was downstairs ready to take him to the meeting. This was it. Hopefully, the beginning of the end.

~~~~~

Thankfully, the doorway was deep so Turner was in the shadows. He wanted to pull the map of the city up on his phone, but couldn't risk the light giving his position away. Instead he waited.

It was deep in the night. He'd had a fruitful meeting with the businessman, and then they'd gone to the reception. Local and foreign dignitaries were in attendance. Many Turner was familiar with, though he hadn't met them. He knew them by reputation and wasn't pleased to make their acquaintance. It made his return to the hotel precarious at best. He hadn't wanted to be dependent on his business contact to do so.

As he'd surmised, he'd been searched when he entered the meeting. The Sig Sauer had been removed from his shoulder holster. His contact seemed pleased that Turner had been carrying. They didn't search him further. A fact which he was glad of.

Rather than sit, Turner chose to walk around the room as they discussed. When asked why, he said flying always left him restless, so he preferred to pace rather than sit.

Papers were scattered on several tables. All were in Arabic. As he rounded the room, Turner blinked taking photos from various angles. When he delivered them the images would be blended, then the text translated so the information could be extracted. That wasn't his concern. He only needed to gather the intel.

As the reception was coming to a close, Turner excused himself and headed to the restroom. He didn't want to accept any of the offers to take him back to his hotel. When he exited the small room, he saw a head dart back behind a corner. Yes, he was being followed.

Panic, residual effects of his kidnapping, threatened to close his throat. He swallowed down the fear. He'd been trained for this situation. Just follow protocol, keep alert and he should be able to get back to the hotel safely. He added one more action to the list: pray.

As he stood listening in the shadowed doorway, Turner gave a wry grin. Here he was in a Muslim country praying fervently to the Christian God.

He took a moment and removed the brass knuckles from his hand, putting them into the exterior breast pocket. He'd zipped his jacket clear to his chin when he exited the building where the reception was. That concealed him in the darkness of the street since his pants were also black. Not even the white of his shirt color was visible.

Turner had taken down the man who was waiting in the hallway for him. The brass knuckles had made that easy. Then he'd slipped down a staircase used by the staff and out into an alley behind the building. Now he was making his way across the city. Once he came to a spot he could hide and wait, one that he could identify to the driver, Turner would call for pick up.

Listening intently, Turner eased to the edge of the doorway. He looked out around the edge and pulled his head back in. The street was dark, only dimly lit by a few streetlights, most of which were burned out, and some light coming from windows. Little moonlight made it past the roofs of the buildings crowded together. He wasn't in the best part of town. No one seemed around.

He backed up into the doorway. Taking out his phone, he quickly pulled up the image of the map. One of the circled places was about four blocks away. Maybe it could offer somewhere for him to hide and call the driver.

He peered out again. Still no one. He prayed it would stay that way. Turner took off at a quick jog. The rubber soles of his shoes padding softly on the surface of the street.

A hand grabbed at him from another doorway, clasping his right arm. Something was said in Arabic. Turner lifted his left hand which now held the ceramic knife and slashed the wrist that held him. A stifled scream of pain. His arm was released. A quick kick of his foot. A chop with his right hand. His assailant dropped.

Turner ran down the narrow street not looking back, trying to keep his footfalls quiet. Between the dim gleaming of the pale buildings one stood out. It was a gray tower. A broken-down wire fence enclosed it. Without much effort, Turner climbed over. The door was set at an angle to the street, shadowed by the tower. A keyed padlock secured it.

Pulling the lock pick kit from his sleeve, Turner made short work of opening the lock. The door squeaked a bit as he pushed it open only far enough for him to enter. He set the lock so a casual glance would make it appear still locked, then slipped into the tower.

No windows in the walls kept any light from entering. He took out his phone and activated the flashlight. There wasn't anything but a few rags, dry leaves and a staircase that hugged the curve of the tower as it ascended. Keeping the light pointed at the stairs, Turner climbed to the top room of the tower.

Moonlight shone in the glassless window. There was a counter or desk along the wall. Remnants of wires and rusted pipes stuck out. Turner looked out the window. The tower had a great view of the shoreline. It struck him that the place where he stood had been a radio tower from World War II.

Suddenly the place didn't seem like a safe haven. The thought of taking refuge in a former Nazi lookout tower sat ill on his shoulders.

Turner sent the text to his driver as quickly as he could. It wasn't long before a reply chirped in. Ten minutes later the sound of a scooter approaching sent him down the stairs. With a cautious look out the door, Turner slipped out, locked the door and climbed onto the back of the scooter.

~~~~~

Turner flopped down into the airplane seat. He was exhausted. After they'd gotten back to the hotel, the driver had told him to get packed. He'd take Turner straight to the airport. There was no way he could stay in Casablanca even overnight. He'd be back in fifteen minutes with a car to take Turner to the airport.

Packing his suitcase quickly, Turner also packed the Pico and lock pick set in the small black case. He'd take it with him to the car and leave it there when he got out. The trick was getting home.

Once Turner was at the airport, he purchased a ticket to Barcelona, Spain. He went through security, then back out to the ticketing counters again and purchased another ticket, this time to Nice, France. He also bought an English newspaper just as the newsstand opened. Using the Barcelona ticket, he went through security again but went to the gate for the Nice flight. That flight was leaving in ten minutes. Just as he was heading onto the jet bridge to board, he looked back and saw several men dressed in black hurry past the gate. He didn't take an easy breath until the jet was speeding down the runway, and the wheels lifted off the ground.

In a restroom stall in the Nice airport, Turner took out his phone. He downloaded the audio files and images recorded while he was at the meeting and reception onto a micro SD card. He had no clue whether he'd recorded anything on his run through the alleys or when he was in the tower. From his pocket, he took a nickel. Twisting it open, he placed the SD card in the hollow cavity and closed the coin. It could stay in his pocket since he was inside security. He'd deliver it when he arrived in the U.S.

At Nice, he'd booked a flight to London with a connection to the States. Now, five hours later he was on the transatlantic flight. Turner breathed a sigh. Last time he had flown this direction, from Tel Aviv, he'd been exhausted too. He needed to decide if he wanted the meal or just to go to sleep. He sent texts to Kyria and Noelle saying he was on his way. Turner thought about typing his report, but fell asleep before the jet pulled away from the gate.

Finally, Turner was back in Benton. He'd gone through customs in New York and taken a commuter jet for the last leg of his journey. As he exited the jet bridge, he saw his contact sitting at the gate across the corridor. He walked part way toward the exit, then stood leaning against the wall.

Turner reached into his pocket and retrieved the nickel. He stood flicking it up and catching it, his phone in his other hand against his ear. Within a few minutes his contact walked by, grabbing the coin from the air as he passed. Turner completed the motion of catching and then stuck his hand in his pocket. He stood away from the wall, put his phone in his jacket pocket, took hold of the handle of his roller bag, and continued on his way to the exit.

CHAPTER ELEVEN

Turner was on his way back. Noelle was pleased he'd texted to let her know, but her doubts weren't eased. She was a little surprised that his trip had been so short. She tried to figure the time changes and what the schedule for his meetings might have been, but it was beyond her.

All she knew was that Turner wanted to see her and the boys that evening. He planned to bring pizza to her house for supper. He'd asked whether they wanted, *Like spinach, artichoke, and vegan cheese pizza.* Then, a moment later, *LOL* came through. That made her smile. Turner had a good sense of humor and didn't take himself too seriously.

She knew Kyria hadn't been pleased with her brother because of his long absence from her life. Then he'd shown up when he found out she was getting married. They'd had a huge fight that Mark had to break up.

Turner admitting his being in the wrong at not keeping in contact with his sister, and his subsequent change, impressed Noelle. Kyria was delighted. After the rocky start, Mark had become good friends with

Turner also. Neither Kyria nor Mark complained about his living with them while he was in town. Seems he even did his own laundry.

His suggestion of how to deal with her team, and the sets and props for the Christmas play had been very successful too. At least for the most part. She was getting emails outlining the progress various team members were making several times a week. There were a couple of people she hadn't heard from. Their responsibilities, she was preparing for a last minute push to get it done. Noelle mentally kicked herself for not thinking of emailing her team before.

Still, Noelle had reservations about Turner. Sure, he made her and her sons feel important to him. He texted her daily even if he didn't come over. When he was at the house, he played with the boys. She grinned. Maybe he was taking advantage of the opportunity to play with kids that he hadn't had as a boy.

"What are you smiling about?" Asked one of her co-workers. Noelle was in the break room eating her lunch.

"Just thinking about a friend and how he plays with the boys when he's over."

"He?" another one asked. "Spill, girl. You dating?"

Rats, thought Noelle. She hadn't mentioned Turner and really didn't want their relationship to become fodder for the office gossip mill. No help for it now. "You know about my friend Kyria? Her brother's in town for the holidays. I met him at the Harvest Hop. He comes over some and plays with the boys. They love the attention."

"So the boys are the draw, huh?"

Noelle felt her cheeks flush. Laughter from her co-workers filled the room. "Well, I might be of slight interest to him."

"Okay, I know you have a photo. Give me your phone."

Noelle scooped it up from the table. The last thing she wanted was for them all to see the text messages they'd shared. Not that there was anything wrong with any of them. She just wanted to keep them to herself.

"Here he is." She pulled up a photo she'd taken of Turner and the boys playing on the floor. He was lying on his back with Mace sitting on his chest, and Camden sprawled across his legs. They were all looking at her with huge smiles on their faces.

"Shut up. He's way cute."

Her phone was passed around the table, each person flipping back and forth through the images to see whether there were any more.

"You haven't taken any selfies with him."

"Don't sound so disappointed. There are plenty of him."

"Yeah, with the boys. How come there aren't any with you?"

Noelle shrugged. She wasn't going to say they had been texted to her and she hadn't moved them to her photo app.

"What's his name?"

"Turner."

"Humph. First or last?"

"First."

"You gonna give us his last name?"

"Nope, if I do, you'll go Google him, and I don't want you to."

"Secretive much?" There was a touch of hurt in the

voice.

Noelle felt bad that she wasn't confiding in her co-workers, but wasn't going to be forced to give more information than she wanted. "Look, I don't know if this relationship will go anywhere. He's just here for the holidays. Next year?" She lifted a shoulder. "I'm concerned enough about the boys becoming too attached to Turner and him leaving after the first of the year. Brad's not much of a father. They don't need to lose another man from their life."

The teasing expressions around the table turned serious. Several heads nodded. They understood Noelle's worry. Each woman would put her children's welfare above her own love life.

~~~~~

Turner could tell something was wrong. Noelle hadn't been herself that evening. Or at least it seemed so to him. Though she'd been pleased to see him come into the great room, carrying several pizza boxes, her eyes didn't sparkle at seeing him like they had before. Both boys welcomed him with open arms. Or maybe closed arms, as Mace had hugged him when he opened the front door to let Turner in.

The boys wanted him to help put them to bed, so after they'd changed into their PJs, Turner supervised the teeth brushing. He'd stood in the doorway and watched as Noelle prayed with each one. Then he'd excused himself, using the excuse that he needed to use the restroom. Now, he was pouring two glasses of wine as he waited for her to come from the boys' room.

When he'd landed earlier that day, the first thing he'd done was to send off his report. Turner definitely wasn't happy about what had happened in Morocco. He'd let his contact know. He'd also requested twenty-four/seven security for Kyria, Mark, his extended family, and Noelle and the boys. It had been approved for his sister and husband only.

Once he'd rung off, he arranged for the security he wanted for the others. He'd make sure they were all safe while this thing was going down. The last thing he wanted was more deaths, especially more of those he loved.

Turner had scanned the house with his phone's app that located bugs and cameras. His heart had eased when none were discovered. He'd done the same at Kyria's house when he stopped by there to change clothes.

He took a sip of wine. He might as well admit it to himself. He was in love with Noelle. Loved just about everything about her. That she let others take advantage of her wasn't the greatest, but he was sure there were things about him she didn't like. He knew she didn't like his trips abroad. Maybe if he could tell her more about them, she would accept them better.

He knew she worried that he'd abandon her and her sons after the holidays were over. Why wouldn't she? He'd blown into town only expecting to spend a couple of months then blow back out, only coming back when he wanted. Or until the project was complete. Until that happened, he was at the beck and call of others.

As much as he wanted to make plans for the future, at the moment, he couldn't. Something larger than his desire was coming. After what had happened in Morocco, he might not have a future to plan.

Noelle came into the great room. Her eyes were large

and haunted. Turner prayed she didn't ask him to leave and not return. He knew he couldn't do that. He also knew he wouldn't tell her of his love for her. Not until he knew how this whole thing would end, or maybe that it simply was finished. Whether it succeeded or failed, it would be over soon. Turner prayed he wouldn't have to travel again, but deep in his gut he knew he would.

"I need to know, Turner. You aren't going to hurt my boys, are you? Just up and disappear after the holidays? If you think that might be the case, then I want you to leave now and not come back. Their father is distancing himself more and more each week. I'm not sure he'll be around much in the future. I won't have them coming to love you, and expect yours back, only to have them hurt by you abandoning them."

Turner set the wine glass on the counter. He knew it would taste bitter if he drank any.

"I'd never knowingly hurt you or the boys." He swallowed the words he wanted to say. Now wasn't the time. There was too much uncertainty. Morocco had proven that. "I'm hoping I won't have to travel again, but most likely will. I don't want to. I will if I'm asked though.

"Just know this. Nothing will keep me from being here, in Benton, by your side, if I am able. Nothing."

"Turner, you're scaring me. What is this project you're involved in? Surely you have enough money that a business deal failing wouldn't affect you that much."

Turner wrapped his arms around her and held her tightly to him. He never wanted to leave her again. "I do. If this was just a business deal, I would have abandoned it long ago."

CHAPTER TWELVE

Noelle got a call from the director of the Christmas play while she was at work. She returned it during her lunch break. Two of the sets weren't ready and quite a few props hadn't been supplied. He was upset. The first dress rehearsal had been difficult without the props. He threatened to call Hutch.

"Go ahead. I've kept him aware of the struggles I've had with some of the team members not doing their part. Maybe if you let him know how difficult you had it last night, he'll finally allow me to relieve some members of their responsibility. Or better yet, he'll do it himself.

"All that said, email me which sets are needing to be done, and a list of the missing props. I'll be sure they are ready by your next rehearsal."

She ended the call and sighed. Just what she needed to fit into her schedule; to paint another couple of sets. Kyle Devaney seemed to enjoy it. Maybe he'd be willing to help again. She pulled up Liam's contact information on her phone and called. With some juggling of schedules and plans, Kyle was going to meet her at church after supper. Noelle hated the thought of making the boys sit around while she painted the sets. It was bad enough that she had to. Maybe?

With only a few minutes left before she went back to work, Noelle called Turner.

"Hi, I'm surprised you called. Aren't you at work?"

"Yes, on my lunch break. I have a favor to ask." She explained the problem then, took a breath before making her request. "Would you be willing to stay with the boys this evening? I can make supper, and then you can get them ready for bed. I shouldn't be very late, I don't think."

"How about I make it even easier for you? I'll pick them up from their after-school program, if you'll let the authorities know to allow me to. Then I'll take them Christmas shopping and buy them supper. We'll be home by seven so I can get them ready for bed. That will relieve you of all responsibility for them until you kiss them goodnight."

Noelle nearly cried. He was such a great guy. "You'd do that?"

"Of course. Besides, how are your guys supposed to get you a Christmas gift unless someone besides you takes them?"

"You're sweet for doing this. Camden has a key to the house attached inside his book bag. Thanks so much. I have to go. I'll call the after-school program right away. You won't have any trouble picking them up."

"Have fun painting, Sweetheart." Turner ended the call.

Noelle was talking with the after-school program director to allow Turner to get the boys, when a message chirped. When she finished the call, she looked at it.

If there's anything you want for Christmas, let me know.
Also, if there are props needed, send me a list. We can pick them
up while we shop.

This man was definitely a keeper. She hadn't even mentioned the props. If only she didn't have doubts about his project and the travel it involved.

~~~~~

Camden and Mace were excited to have Turner pick them up from their school, where the after-school program was held in the gym. The supervising teacher had informed them that he was coming. They ran across the room when Turner entered. When they found out they were going to the mall for supper and to shop for their mother, the boys fist bumped and high fived all the way to Turner's Macan.

"Cool, we get to ride in your purple car," Mace bounced along the sidewalk, holding onto Turner's hand.

"It's iris, not purple."

Camden studied the vehicle while Turner got the booster seats out of the cargo space and opened the back door. "No, I think it really is purple." His serious contemplation had Turner smothering a laugh.

"Hop in and buckle up."

As they entered the mall, Mace said, "I'm hungry. Can we get a snack?"

There was a hot pretzel shop giving off a welcoming, mouth-watering aroma. Turner was pulled along by his hands, and was soon ordering three pretzels along with a couple of dipping sauces and lemonades. He was smart enough to sit them at a small table so the mess and crumbs were scattered in a limited space.

"We're gonna buy Mommy presents for Christmas and her birthday, right?" Camden asked, his gaze focused on a pop-up shop in the middle of the mall fairway called 'Every Gift Under $5.' The display held bins of small items in bright colors that appealed to small boys, maybe girls, too, but he had boys to deal with.

"Yes, since her birthday is so close to Christmas, today would be a good day to get presents for both. That way we don't have to go shopping again."

"That's good," said Mace, his mouth full of pretzel.

"Do you have any ideas about what you think she might like?" Turner asked.

Neither boy said anything. They just kept looking at the kiosk. Turner decided it would be their first stop.

As he threw their trash away, Mace and Camden ran to inspect the offerings. By the time Turner caught up with them, each held something they wanted to give their mom. Mace had on a pair of over-sized googley eyeglasses. Camden was wearing small plastic feet on his fingers, walking them along the edge of the bins.

"She'll love these," Mace said peering through the tiny holes in the glasses, the black 'pupils' bouncing as he jerked his head around. Turner doubted it, but was going to buy them anyway.

"These are cool. Finger feet. See?" Camden walked his feet clad fingers up Turner's arm.

They walked around to the other side. Both boys stopped and reached for the same thing; long dangly, fuzzy feather earrings in neon pink.

"Oooo. She'll look great in these." Camden lifted the card they were attached to carefully.

"They'd be perfect for her birthday. It's after

Christmas so she could wear them right away." Mace touched a finger to the fluff.

Turner bit the inside of his cheek to keep from laughing. They were so serious, wanting to buy things Noelle would like. Not that she would, but she'd love each and every gift. It was the thought that counted anyway, especially with children.

Their purchases made, Turner herded them past the shops. He wanted to get something somewhat nicer for her. Plus he had a couple of items to get at the cycle shop for himself. The boys would love looking at all the gear hanging on the walls.

"Look." Mace pointed at the window of a gift shop. "I think we should get her that." He pressed up against the glass. Camden ran to stand next to him.

Turner chuckled. They were getting into the spirit of the mouse thing. "Okay, but does she have any plants? That's a mouse watering can."

"No," said Camden, "but that doesn't matter. It's a mouse."

"Can we get it?" Mace looked up at him, worry and pleading in his eyes.

"Sure. We can even get a fake plant to put in it. Maybe they have one in here we can buy. Come on."

Turner led the way into the shop, and soon they exited with a bag containing a teal mouse watering can with an arrangement of orange flowers tucked inside.

In the cycle shop Turner let the boys wander with the admonition to not touch anything as he spoke with the clerk. He was concluding his purchase when Mace pulled on his sleeve.

"Yes?"

"We found something we want to get for Mommy.

We can take some of the other things back if you want us to. This is really cool."

Turner wondered what they'd found for Noelle here. She wasn't into cycling, that he knew of. He followed Mace to where Camden was standing next to a display of SPF sleeves. Most were white, black, or light blue. Some were multicolored. Others were covered with tattoo designs. He wondered which attracted the boys. He hoped it wasn't the skulls or pin-up girls.

"You know what these are for?" He asked.

"To protect you from the sun?" Camden said a little doubtfully.

"Yes, when you cycle long distances the sun can burn you terribly. With these you don't have to keep applying sunscreen. They keep you warm or cool too. Which one are you interested in for your mom?"

Two hands pointed to a brightly colored sleeve with flowers and a bird that looked a little like a sea horse. He grinned. "I think she'd like that."

"She'd look real pretty with those on her arms. She gets cold easy. They could keep her warm," Mace said.

Turner signaled Camden that he could take one set down. He pulled out his wallet and handed the boy some money. "Here, you go pay for this."

The grin on Camden's face spread wide. He marched to the counter and made the transaction. Turner and Mace stood a few steps back watching.

"Can I buy the next thing?" Mace asked. "I know something she needs."

"Oh? What?"

"Deodorant. She said she needed to buy more soon. There's a discount store that way." Mace pointed. "We can get it next."

Again, Turner bit his cheek. Noelle was in for surprises on Christmas morning and her birthday, with what her sons were buying for her.

Across from the entrance to the discount store was a high-end ladies lingerie shop. Though the boys wanted to go in and find something for their mother, Turner decided that just might be crossing the line for him to purchase something so intimate. Instead, he noticed a candy store and persuaded them to get her something there. They chose white chocolate covered pretzel wands with multi-colored sprinkles. Seems they liked pretzels very much.

By now the boys were hungry and getting bored with shopping. The food court took care of the appetite with corndogs and French fries. Turner wasn't sure Noelle would approve of the junk food supper, but he'd ask forgiveness if it was needed.

"Now," he said. "We need to find one more thing for her, and I have an idea. Come on, guys."

Turner led the way to a store that sold watches. There were all types. He went to a counter with novelty watches and surveyed the offerings.

"There." He pointed at one. It was a Mickey Mouse watch. "It even plays the Mickey Mouse Club song."

Mace and Camden began singing, "Hot dog, hot dog, hot diggity dog."

"No, not that one. The real one. 'Who's the leader of the club that's made for you and me.' That one."

"Man, you're really old. That's in black and white," Mace said.

"There are some in color too. Anyway, she could use this at work since it has a second hand. See?" Turner pointed to the watch face.

"Yeah, and it's big so it's easy to see. She doesn't like little bitty watches," Camden said.

Mace nodded.

"So, shall we get it for her as your last gift? It goes along with our mouse theme."

While Turner paid for the watch, Camden and Mace sang the hot dog version they knew.

~~~~~

Turner collapsed on the sofa. He was exhausted. Camden and Mace were finally in bed. He hoped they would go to sleep. He looked at his watch. Noelle hadn't called or texted that she was on her way home yet, so he still had some time to clean up. Bits of wrapping paper, ribbon, bows, tags, and tape were scattered and stuck to the kitchen table.

At the discount store, he'd purchased the wrapping supplies, and the three of them had wrapped all the gifts. Turner looked at the two piles of presents; one wrapped in Christmas paper, the other in birthday. They looked like they'd been wrapped by a six and four-year-old. Some Noelle would have difficulty opening since they were covered in yards of tape.

There were scraps of paper all over the floor. They'd had so much fun cutting the paper and wrapping the gifts, and were so very proud of the results. Turner had enjoyed it too.

His phone chirped. Checking the message, he stood and stretched. Noelle was on her way home. He texted a thumbs up and began to clean up the mess.

Turner had just stuffed the last of the trash into the wastebasket when Noelle came in through the door to the garage. He smiled at her, but it faded at her sour expression.

"Um, bad night?"

Noelle set her keys on the hook beside the door and dropped her purse on the small table under it. "Not the greatest day either. As I was leaving work, Alene Dufflemeyer saw me heading to my car. She told me how disappointed she was that I didn't have my committee well organized. They didn't have the sets and props all ready for the dress rehearsal last night.

"She didn't mention that her daughter was one who didn't get hers completed. I called her on it. I told her that Mary Sue, that's her daughter, was one who hadn't gotten her sets done or any of the props on her list.

"Told her Hutch was pretty upset that she hadn't even opened most of the emails I sent out." Noelle removed her coat and hung it in the closet. "'Well,' she said. 'I'm sure she didn't receive them. You must have the wrong email address.' I told her it was the one in the church directory. The one we got last month so it was up to date.

"Also, I set the emails to let me know when they were opened. Hers never were. 'You can do that?'" Noelle said the last words in the nasal tones of Alene Dufflemeyer. "She was shocked. It's pretty simple. Just a setting within the email program."

"I know."

"She stormed away after that." Noelle accepted the bottle of water Turner offered to her, cracking it open and taking a long drink.

"It got worse after Brad called. We got both sets painted and most of the props rounded up. I texted the other team members, who came through and found most of the items. Only about half a dozen left. They are all accounted for by various members of the team.

That's why I didn't send you the list."

"That's good." He walked over to her and pulled her into his arms. "Now, what's wrong?"

Noelle gave a huge sigh. "As I said, Brad called. He can't take the boys on Wednesday. He and Kim have plans." She dropped her forehead onto his chest. "He's even starting to talk like her. Just about every other word is 'like.' 'We, like, have plans to, like, go to a hockey game. Like, can't take the boys there.' Makes me want to puke."

"How he talks or that he won't take the boys?"

"Humph, both." She looked up at him. "How'd it go for you tonight? Did they wear you out?"

Turner chuckled. "Just about. No wonder you're so tired all the time. Working all day, then having those bundles of energy. We had a good time. Got you presents for Christmas and your birthday. They are positive you'll love every single one of them."

Noelle frowned at him. "How many did you get and how much did you spend?"

"Nine total, but nothing was very expensive. There are even two very practical gifts. You even told Mace you needed one of them."

"Oh?"

"Yeah, it's one you will get on Christmas since that comes first. He wants to be sure you have it." He turned her to face the table. "See, we even wrapped them."

Noelle went over and picked up each one, shaking them next to her ear. "Only one rattles a little. Wow, that's a lot of tape. I'll need scissors or a knife to cut it open."

"Mace wanted to be sure the paper held, and that

you couldn't peek."

"Well, they succeeded. No way could I peel any paper back on that." She set the gift down. "Why doesn't Brad want his sons? I know I'm not what he wants, but how do I explain to Camden and Mace that, once again, their dad doesn't want to be with them? I don't want them to think it's them or their fault. I also don't want to bad-mouth Brad. He is their father."

Turner stood behind her and wrapped his arms around her waist, setting his chin on her head. "I wish I had the answer. Maybe speak with Hutch about it. He might know a way to give balance."

CHAPTER THIRTEEN

"Your boys insist my Macan is purple," Turner said as he opened the passenger door for Noelle.

"It is."

"It's iris. Says so on the window sticker."

"Don't care. It's purple."

He shut the door as she buckled her seat belt. They were going to the mall to go Christmas shopping. Brad had the boys over the weekend, so Noelle thought it was the perfect time to get her shopping done. Turner had his shopping completed, so he was going to advise her on what four and six-year-old boys would want. After all, he'd been both. When he told her that, she grinned a little.

Noelle wanted to just rush through the mall, getting the things on her list as quickly as possible. Turner had other ideas. He held her hand and strolled slowly down the fairway, pointing out anything that might be of the slightest interest to her. When they went into the various department stores, he guided her through the ladies sections.

"Why are we going through here? I only need to go to the boys department. They both need jeans."

Noelle's frustration was evident in her tone.

"Because you need to relax. We have all day. No need to rush. Just enjoy looking at the clothes and other things we see."

"But I want to get all the presents wrapped before the boys get home."

Turner turned her to face him and placed his hands on her shoulders. He studied the serious expression on her face. Something had to be done to get her into the holiday spirit. "They aren't coming home until tomorrow evening. There's time. If it's going to cause you to not enjoy doing the shopping, we'll have them gift wrapped here in the mall. There's a high school band or team or club raising money by doing gift wrapping. We can support them. I'll pay.

"Let's just have fun doing the shopping you want and looking at the people and the consumerism that Christmas has become."

Noelle's shoulders relaxed, and she let a small smile pull at her lips. "You're right. I'm letting the stress of work, the church program, and Brad take all the joy out of my life." She took a deep breath and let it whoosh out of her lungs. "Okay, show me what you want, but we do need to get jeans for the boys."

Rather than hold her hand, Turner put his arm around her shoulders. "Come on. Let's look at the Christmas displays they have. Who knows? You might find something you want to hang on your tree."

They wandered through the racks and rows, past gift idea items that only seemed to come out during the holiday. Nearly out of the holiday section, Turner saw something and stopped. "Come on. We have to get some."

"What?"

Turner pulled her along, rushing to a table piled high. "Ugly Christmas sweaters. We can get matching ones. Do you suppose they have them in Camden's and Mace's sizes? Wouldn't it be sweet for us to all wear matching ones to the Jenners on Christmas?"

The appalled look on Noelle's face gave him the answer, but he wasn't going to allow it to deter him. He grabbed one off the table and held it up. "Look, it's a present, complete with a gold bow."

"It certainly is." Noelle flipped the large 3-D gold ribbon attached right in the center of the sweater front.

"OOO, here's a great one." He dropped the present sweater and picked up another one. It was blue with a large Christmas tree on the front. Red, white, and gold glittery pompons decorated the tree and ran up black suspenders. He held it up in front of his chest. "How great is this?"

Turner finally got the reaction from Noelle he wanted; her lips curled up in a smile. Glancing at a table behind her, he dashed over and grabbed one, plunking it on his head. "See, there's even a matching hat."

Noelle started laughing. "You're a doofus, you know that?" She reached up and swiped the stuffed tree hat off his head. She put it back on the table, took the sweater from him, folded it, and placed it on the stack.

"Does this mean we aren't going to get ugly Christmas sweaters?" He tried to sound like a disappointed little boy.

"You can certainly buy one, but if you want to be seen with me, you won't ever wear it when I'm with you."

"Spoilsport. Ugly Christmas sweaters are a holiday tradition."

"One that should be retired."

"Okay." Turner hung his head and shuffled away as if he was pouting. He didn't want Noelle to see the pleased grin on his face. He'd gotten her to laugh. He would even have bought the sweaters and worn his if she'd wanted to.

As the day progressed, they found and purchased the things on her list. They had taken the gifts to be wrapped and had lunch, then later in the afternoon shared an ice cream sundae.

Turner carried most of the bags as they left the mall, with Noelle only having a few. They were going to eat out at a new steak restaurant. Night was falling, and the parking lot was crowded with people and moving vehicles.

Noelle stumbled against Turner as she was pushed from behind. At the same time, the bags he was carrying were ripped from one hand as a mugger ran past. Another grabbed the bags Noelle carried.

Turner dropped his other bags and took off running after the men. One dashed between two cars. The other wasn't quite as fast. Turner caught up with him and slammed his head against an SUV. He dropped. Noelle ran up beside Turner.

He pulled a Taser from a pocket under the sleeve of his jacket "You hold this on him. If he moves an eyelash, Tase him." He flipped up a tab on the side seam of his jacket and pulled out a long zipper tie. "Use this to cuff him." Then, he took off running after the other man. "Call 911," he yelled back.

Being tall, Turner could see over many of the

vehicles. He spotted the mugger in the next parking row. He was running but was also having to fit the shopping bags between the cars, which slowed him down. Turner wasn't so encumbered. He could tell he was gaining on the man.

Fortunately, no cars were coming as Turner ran through the next lane. He crossed at a slight diagonal to better align himself with the mugger. The man made a poor choice as he went between a van and a tall truck. Turner gritted his teeth as the thief crashed over a stroller with a toddler in it, tumbling to the ground. The child started crying, the mother screamed, Turner slid around the stroller and placed his knee on the mugger's back, pinning him to the asphalt.

"Call 911, please," Turner said to the woman who was getting her child out of the stroller. When he saw she was doing so, Turner flipped open the tab on the seam of his jacket and pulled out another long, plastic zipper tie. Pulling the man's arms behind him, he secured the hands of his captive.

"Are you a policeman?" the woman asked.

"No, but I've had some training."

Sirens could be heard approaching. A mall security squad came up the lane and stopped close by. Two officers got out.

"What's going on?" one asked.

"This man and one other ran past me and my girlfriend, grabbing our bags. I downed one, and chased after and caught this one." Turner stood. "He'd tripped over this woman's stroller."

"You downed one?" the officer looked suspiciously at him.

"Knocked him against a car. My girlfriend is holding

a Taser on him. Over there, three more rows over." Turner pointed and saw another set of flashing lights near where he'd left Noelle.

A city police car came up the aisle from the other direction. It didn't take long for their statements to be taken and the thief to be placed in the back of the squad car. "You'll need to come to the station either tonight or tomorrow to complete the paperwork."

"I have one more question," the mall security officer said.

Turner looked at him.

"You make a habit of carrying long zipper ties with you?"

Turner grinned at him. "You'd be surprised how often one or more comes in handy. It did tonight."

He gathered the shopping bags and went back to where Noelle was still talking with the police officer, who now had the mugger sitting against the SUV Turner had smashed him against.

"This is Turner Metcalf. He's the man who stopped this one." She pointed to the man lying on the ground.

Turner answered the questions the police officer asked, repeating what he'd told the other one. Just as they were finishing, a TV camera van turned into the lane.

"Look," Turner said to the officer. "We'll come down to the station after we have some supper. Maybe about two hours. Will that be okay?"

"That'll be fine."

Turner glanced at the reporter and camera man who were getting out of the van. "I don't want to be interviewed or on TV. Will you let us get out of here? You can tell them anything but my name. Tell them we want to remain anonymous, or that Noelle is too upset to be on camera. Maybe they'd want to speak with the woman whose stroller was tripped over. That's what allowed me to capture the man."

"You have some reason you don't want to be identified as the man who finally ended the mall muggers' series of thefts?"

"Yes, I can explain it when we are down at the station. I just need to get out of here before they splash my image all over the TV." While he was talking, he pulled a stocking cap from his pocket and covered his hair with it. Noelle was gathering the bags. The policeman nodded and waved at his partner, who went to intercept the TV crew.

"I'll be interested in your story." The officer's tone held skepticism.

Turner placed his hand on Noelle's back and gently guided her away from the scene. A crowd had gathered, and Turner used all his experience to navigate them through and to his car. They were silent as they put the bags in the Macan. Turner helped Noelle into her seat and went around and got in.

"How…" Noelle began.

"Not yet. Let's go get a quick bite to eat rather than a heavy meal. Then we can go to the police station and finish up the report."

He glanced at Noelle who nodded. He didn't like the distressed look on her face.

~~~~~

Noelle watched Turner drive out of the corner of her eye. They'd decided to go to a local sports themed restaurant where the meal wouldn't take as long. The day's enjoyment had been squashed by the attempted mugging.

Who was this man who was concentrating on the road so fiercely? She knew he'd trained in martial arts. He'd mentioned that when he told her of the kidnapping he'd suffered as a child. But to have a Taser and zipper ties in that jacket of his? What was that about?

Noelle thought about what he'd either told her he carried, or she'd seen. The Velcro straps to hold his jeans legs out of the bike. That was understandable. A deck of cards. Okay, a bit odd, but it had come in handy to entertain the boys while she cleaned up at the Harvest Hop. She remembered a comment he'd made at the time; 'You'd be surprised what I have on me at all times.'

He'd pulled the Taser from some hidden pocket, she was sure. Just where had that been stored? And zipper ties long enough to handcuff someone?

She turned her head to look at him. "Are you carrying a concealed weapon?" When his shoulders seemed to slump just a bit, she had her answer.

He sighed. "Yes. I always have a weapon."

Noelle noted he didn't identify what type. "A gun?"

"Usually."

"Now?"

"Yes, among others."

"You're packing not only a gun, but other weapons?"

He didn't answer. He just turned into the parking lot of the restaurant. Once Turner had parked the car and turned the engine off, he shifted in his seat so he faced her.

"Noelle, I've been kidnapped, I told you that. It

leaves a lasting impression on a person. Maybe there's a bit of PTSD involved. There have been other threats throughout the years. I'm not going to allow myself to be vulnerable ever again. I'm going to do what I can to protect myself and those I love."

Noelle's heart skipped a beat. No, that wasn't a declaration. He was just stating a fact of his life. He would have done the takedown and chase no matter whom he'd been with. It all seemed like natural reflex for him. The speed and fluid motions spoke of acute muscle memory from long hours of training.

Turner reached out and touched her cheek. "Let's go get something to eat and head to the station. I'd like to get the interviews and reports done before it gets too late."

Noelle nodded.

Once they were seated, she excused herself to go to the restroom. When she was returning to the table, she saw Turner on his cell phone. As he saw her approaching the table, Turner ended the call and tucked the phone into the inside breast pocket of his jacket.

Though she'd noticed some oddly placed pockets before, Noelle had assumed they were for style rather than function. She realized each one might just have a tool or weapon in it. The jacket might even have concealed pockets she couldn't tell were there. The zipper ties were evidence of that.

The waitress came and took their orders. Trying to relax, Noelle glanced at the various televisions scattered around the restaurant. One caught her attention.

"Oh, look. There's more news about that country in

Africa. You know, the one with that terrible dictator."

Turner sharply swiveled in his chair and looked at the screen. Closed captioning was activated, so they could read the reporter's words.

"Another village was discovered with all the citizens murdered, right down to a newborn. The bodies were left to rot in the heat. Written in the dirt, next to one of the bodies, was the name 'Atul,' leading UN peace keepers to believe the murders were at the orders of the country's dictator, Demar Atul."

Noelle glanced at Turner as the reporter continued his statements. Turner's jaw was set in a firm line. His expression a mixture of disgust, fury, determination, and hate. Then, he seemed to shake them all off. When he looked at her, it was with sadness and resignation.

"That's such a tragic situation. There doesn't seem to be much that can be done about it. The UN certainly can't get the man ousted."

Noelle nodded. He was right on all points. She looked at the TV again. "Oh, there we are."

Turner jerked around, staring at the screen. Noelle's and his backs were shown walking away from the camera. The caption was explaining that the man who had apprehended the suspected mall muggers didn't want to be identified. He had simply told the police he was glad he could help stop the rash of assaults that was blighting the holiday season.

Turner turned and grinned at her. "Did I ever use the word blighting?"

She chuckled. "Of course. I distinctively remember you even spelling it to the policeman to put in his report."

Turner laid his hand over hers which was lying on

the table. "I know this was a trying event, but let's not let it ruin what had been a great day, at least for me."

She flipped her hand so they were palm to palm and gave his a squeeze. "For me too. Until this last part, I haven't relaxed and just had fun in I don't know how long."

~~~~~

Turner pulled the door of the police station open, holding it so Noelle could precede him into the building. He identified them to the receptionist, and they were taken to a room where they waited for whomever would be speaking with them. Soon, a man dressed in plain clothes and the officers from the scene entered.

The plain clothed man spoke. He was older, though still physically fit, with a smattering of gray hair. "I'm Captain Brocket. These officers identified themselves to you at the scene. Have a seat."

Turner nodded to each man as they all settled around a beat up table. Looking back at the captain, he found himself under an acute stare. He leaned back as comfortably as he could in the hard chair. He set his elbows on the arms, steepling fingers together under his chin.

"You, Mr. Metcalf, have some very influential friends. Homeland Security called and requested…" Brocket made air quotes, "that we simply take your statement about the robbery, and not ask for any other information. I'd ask you to explain yourself, but have been forbidden to do so."

Turner felt Noelle's gaze laser onto him. He didn't move or change the passive expression on his face.

"I did a background check on you," Brocket

continued. "Seems you're filthy rich. Have a reputation of a mild playboy and adventure seeker. You've climbed mountains, biked most of the way across Europe and much of China. You travel extensively and attend some of the most prestigious social events all over the globe.

"You've no drug record, and only a couple of speeding tickets, at least here in the U.S. Your only family is a sister who lives here in Benton. You've been in and out of the country several times in the last few weeks and months. You don't seem to have an official occupation or employment. But then with your wealth, you probably don't need one.

"You have extensive martial arts training. I assume that aided you in apprehending our suspects. The one has a mild concussion, by the way. Good take down, I'm told. Did some damage to the vehicle you smashed him against."

"Have the owner send me the bill for whatever repairs are required. I'm the one who damaged it, after all," Turner said.

Brocket nodded. "So, the puzzle, that I'm not supposed to ask you about, is why you didn't want to be interviewed by the reporters? As a rather minor celebrity, why you wouldn't want to be on TV? I'd think someone of your economic stature and social standing would like to be in the spotlight for being the one who saved the Christmas holiday from the mall muggers." He lifted an inquiring eyebrow, but said nothing else.

"Captain, I'm a private man. You'll note in your research that I've never sought publicity. I'm sure you found reference to my kidnapping when I was eleven.

It left scars. I still have nightmares of that incident in my life. No doubt, this event will bring those to the forefront of my mind again. I won't sleep soundly for several weeks."

"I sympathize with your struggles. None of that explains the phone call or your reluctance to be on TV." He lifted a hand. "But, I will respect the request and simply have these proficient officers write up your statements so you can go." He stood to leave the room, then turned back. "Just one more question. Is whatever you're involved in going to mess up my town?"

"Not to my knowledge. I'd tell you if I thought it would."

"Another thing." The chief looked Turner over. "Why is Homeland Security looking out for a rich playboy, anyway?"

Turner just looked at him, saying nothing.

"I get it. One of those questions I shouldn't have asked."

"Probably not."

Noelle was taken to another office to make her report, while he stayed and answered the questions fired at him. About halfway through, Turner realized, when the officer gave him a quizzical look, he was giving more information than required or expected. He was in report mode, but rather than typing it out was speaking it. The detail he was providing was more than a normal witness would ever remember. Inwardly, he shrugged. Might as well go on as he'd started. It would seem even stranger if he stopped now. By finishing in the same manner, the officer would assume he was just detail oriented.

Noelle was waiting for him in the hall when he and the officer exited the room.

"Thank you, both, for coming in and giving your statements. We think both men will plea bargain. They were caught with the goods in hand, so the case most likely won't come to trial. We'll contact you if you will need to testify." The officer led them to the lobby. "Have a Merry Christmas. I know I'm not supposed to say that, but I don't really care."

Turner shook his hand. "You, too. Let's go, Noelle. It's been a trying evening."

He hoped Noelle would just let what the captain had said lie, but as soon as they were out of the parking lot she brought it up.

"Just who did you call that caused them to phone the police and warn them not to ask too many questions? You were on the phone when I came back from the restroom."

"Noelle, please don't ask. It's not something I can talk about. At least not yet. Suffice it to say that it will be over soon."

"It's about this project that causes you to travel so much."

"Well, I do like to travel." He shot her a sheepish grin. "But yes, it concerns the project. Until it's complete I don't want to be seen on any screen: TV, computer or phone."

"Turner, are you in danger?" Worry and concern were thick in her voice.

He sighed. "I could be. I have been for a very long time." He paused, then continued. "Kyria could be, too. It's one reason I'm here. I can protect her better by being in the proximity."

Noelle laid a hand on his arm. "Are the boys and I in danger?"

"Not if I can help it. That's another reason I didn't want us to be on camera. You haven't been identified as someone connected with me. I intend to keep it that way."

Turner pulled the Macan into her driveway and put it in park. "Noelle, I know this all scares you, and I hate that. Know that I've done everything possible to keep all this away from you."

"You've hired security, haven't you?"

Turner dropped his forehead onto the steering wheel. "Yes. I don't think there will be any problems, but I'm not going to take the chance. Kyria, Mark, you, the boys, Hutch and family, the entire Jenner clan. Each has twenty-four/seven coverage. We had people keeping us under surveillance all through the mall, the parking lot and all that went down there, at the restaurant…" his voice trailed off.

"This is big, isn't it? Bigger than I can imagine."

He lifted his head and looked at her. "Yes. I'll understand if you want me to quit coming around. I won't like it, but I will. Just know this. I won't stop the protection detail. Until the project is complete, everything stays in place."

Noelle was silent for a few moments. "I don't want you to stay away. Not from the boys and not from me."

Now it was Turner's time to be silent. Then he said, "Do you have any other questions?"

Noelle nodded. "Does Brad have a security detail?"

"Only when the boys are with him."

"Good."

CHAPTER FOURTEEN

Once again Turner was in the mall. This time he was shopping with Hutch and Mark. They'd roped him into going with them, saying they needed his expert help in purchasing appropriate gifts for their wives. He'd scoffed that, since he didn't have a wife, there was no way he could know the best gifts for them. Neither man thought it was a good enough excuse to avoid the throngs of people crowding the stores. So, here he was, again, trailing along while others sought his inexpert advice on gift choices.

"Hutch," Turner said. He and the pastor were standing in front of a store entrance waiting for Mark to purchase something for his mother.

"Yeah?"

"I want to say thank you. I've been getting a lot out of your sermons. I began going to church only to please Noelle. She wasn't going to spend time with me unless I attended. I could tell. I wasn't eager to go. Kyria had been asking me ever since I came to town, but I wouldn't go."

Hutch chuckled. "That's because she's just your sister."

That made Turner smile. "Yeah, I suppose so. Her spending time with me isn't as appealing as Noelle."

Now Hutch laughed. "That's pretty insulting to Kyria."

"That's not what I mean."

"I know. As you were saying?"

"As a kid, I went to church and gave my life to Christ. Then, when I was at university, I drifted away. Typical young man letting other interests take precedence over my faith. The cares of the world and all that."

"Very good slaughter of the verse, but I understand what you're saying. It's really easy to do, especially when you're young and away from home and parental influence for the first time."

"Not quite my story but close enough. Anyway, you've got a way of bringing the Scripture to life and making it applicable to mine. I'm seeing it as a guide for living and getting through tough times. Dealing with difficult people. You know. I don't need to explain it to you. I just wanted to say I'm learning and have come back to my faith. Thanks."

Hutch laid a hand on Turner's shoulder. "I appreciate you telling me. I'm pleased I could be of help getting you to come back to the Lord."

Mark came out of the store right then, so the topic ended as they headed to another store.

"Guys," Mark said. "I'm thinking of booking a vacation as a surprise for Kyria. We've been so busy with the house and work that it might be nice for us to get away for a week in January. I've got time off, and Kyria can set her own schedule."

Turner and Hutch thought it was a good idea. There

was a travel agency nearby. They entered discussing where the couple could go. January in Benton was cold and snowy. A week in the Caribbean sounded great to all three men.

Mark and Hutch sat at the agent's desk discussing the plans. Turner wandered around looking at the various brochures depicting popular tourist spots. His back was to chairs arranged as a waiting area when he heard familiar voices.

"Oh Braddy, it's such a, like, wonderful idea to have, like, a destination wedding. I'm so, like, glad you thought of it. We can have, like, my parents and some friends."

"So, do you want to have it in, like, the Bahamas, or Virgin Islands?"

Brad's words grated on Turner's nerves. He didn't turn around, not wanting to reveal himself. Listening and gathering information was what he'd trained for. This might not be exactly what his skills were intended to do, but they were coming in handy at the moment.

"Either one is, like, fine with me. I'm glad it will be just us."

"Yes, it's too late notice for Noelle to get the boys passports, though they wouldn't need them for the Virgin Islands, I don't think."

"Let's not go there. I want to have our wedding be, like, all adults."

"I know what you mean. Having the boys around is, like, wearing. They are so active and need so much attention."

"I know. I didn't realize kids were so, like, a nuisance," Kim said in a pouty voice.

"Well, we won't have to worry about it much longer.

I've put in for that transfer to California. My boss thinks I'm, like, a shoe-in for the job. Once we move, we won't have to have them very often."

"Oh, Braddy. That's, like, so good. I can't wait, sunny California."

Turner crushed the brochure in his hand. He marched over to Hutch and tapped him on the shoulder. When Hutch looked up at him, Turner jerked his chin toward the entrance and headed out. Hutch followed.

Turner stormed down the fairway until he came to a hall leading to restrooms. He entered and stopped about halfway down. Hutch soon caught up.

"What's up?"

"Brad was in there with Kim. They, like, are planning a, like, destination wedding. They don't want the boys there and are going to have it too soon for them to be able to get passports. He's also planning on moving to California. Getting a job transfer. That way they won't have to deal with the nuisance which is his sons.

"Hutch, if I'd have stayed another second I would have pounded the man to a pulp. A bloody pulp, literally." Turner was pacing across the hall and back, his hands opening and closing in fists.

"If I wasn't a man of faith, I'd say a few choice words right now." Hutch ran a hand through his hair making it stand on end.

"How am I going to tell Noelle? I knew Brad was pretty much a jerk, but to purposely get transferred so he doesn't have to spend time with his own sons. That's just low."

"Yes, it is. But, Turner," Hutch said. "You aren't going to talk to Noelle about this. I am. I'm more equipped to help her through the emotional upheaval she'd going to have. Besides, I'm her brother. You're a friend."

Turner shot him a speaking stare. "She's more than a friend to me."

"Have you declared anything?"

"No."

"Then you're still in the friend category."

Turner nodded. He wanted to make a declaration, but until the project was complete, he knew he couldn't. "You can tell her and do what you can to keep her together. I'll support her in any way I can. Camden and Mace, also. They'll be hurt, too. That their dad doesn't care about them is about as tough a concept as a kid can go through."

"Yeah. Come on. Mark has to be looking for us." Hutch's phone chirped. He pulled it from his pocket and checked the message. "That's him. Come on. Let's try to enjoy the rest of the evening, before I have to go and break my sister's heart over the louse of her ex-husband again. Besides, I have to get something for Chloe. I haven't got any clue as to what."

~~~~~

Hutch walked up the sidewalk to Noelle's porch. His feet seemed to drag. This was not going to be a fun evening. He'd called her during her lunch break and asked if he could bring Chinese takeout over, and eat supper with her that night. It was Wednesday, and Brad should have the boys. Chloe and Noah were going to a baby shower at the church. He knew Noelle wasn't going as she wasn't close to the mother-to-be.

His sister had jumped at the chance to have her big

brother to herself for a couple of hours. They'd always been close, and she said she missed the heart to heart talks they had when they were young.

Hutch rang the doorbell and heard her running to the front door. It flew open, and Noelle enveloped him in a hug.

"I'm so glad you called and wanted to get together. Sometimes I miss you so much. Come on in."

"I'm not far away. Plus you can always call."

"I know. It's just different from when we lived in the same house. You were in the next room, and we could talk any time."

Hutch chuckled as he set the bags on the kitchen counter. "I seem to remember a bunch of times when you screamed at me to leave you alone."

Noelle laughed. "Yeah, I did a fair amount of that."

Hutch looked at her smiling face. She seemed happy. Happier than he'd seen her in several years. Even before Brad had told her he wanted a divorce, Noelle had been, if not unhappy, simply not happy. Now, she seemed to be. And he was going to snatch that from her. Sometimes he hated being a counselor.

Noelle bustled about getting plates and silverware. He got the containers from the bags and began dishing out the food. They sat at the counter to eat, engaging in a bit of teasing shoving, pretending to be kids again. Hutch didn't want to spoil the evening, but knew he was going to.

Once they'd cleaned up the leftovers and moved to the sofa, Hutch knew it was time to bring up Brad and what Turner had heard them talking about.

"Noelle, there's something I need to talk with you about, and it's not a pleasant subject."

"Mom and Dad are okay?" Fear filled her eyes.

"Yeah, it's nothing like that. Everyone is fine. Chloe and Noah are great. He's this close to walking." He held up his hand with the thumb and forefinger about an inch apart. "Everyone keeps telling me to push him down. Push him down. Once they walk, you are forever chasing them."

"They are right. You can't keep them out of anything once they are mobile." Noelle laughed. Then, she became serious. "What's going on then?"

Hutch swallowed. He didn't want to break her heart, but knew he was going to. "It's about Brad."

Her expression soured. "What about Brad?"

"We, Mark, Turner, and I, were in the mall last night. We'd gone Christmas shopping. Guys helping guys shop for their girls. Mark's going to give Kyria a vacation to Jamaica for Christmas. They'll go in January. We were in the travel agency. Mark and I were at the desk, and Turner was wandering around."

He went on to tell what Turner had overheard. Noelle listened, her back getting straighter and stiffer as he spoke. When he got to the point where Brad called the boys a nuisance, she collapsed against the back of the sofa. Tears were streaking down her face.

"Mace and Camden nuisances? His own sons? How could he?" Noelle covered her face with her hands. When she dropped them, she looked at Hutch. "How am I going to explain to the boys that their father doesn't want them? That he thinks they are a nuisance. They are going to be devastated."

"Camden's probably figured it out already. He may only be six, but they know, even that young, who they are important to. Mace may not, but there is always a chance they have talked about their dad and how they think he feels about them.

"The best thing you can do is be honest."

"You mean I should tell them their dad is a louse who is a total waste of skin?"

Hutch chuckled and pulled her into a hug. "No, Squirt, you tell them that it's not that Daddy doesn't love or want you. He's confused. He's trying to learn how to be a daddy and to be the bimbo's boyfriend, soon-to-be husband."

Noelle chuckled at the term Hutch used.

"He hasn't figured it out yet. We need to give him time. Maybe lots of time. Reassure them that you love them and want them with you. Tell them that Uncle Hutch and Aunt Chloe love them and will visit a lot. Mimi and Papa love them too."

Noelle nodded against his chest. "Have you told them?"

"Mom and Dad? No. I will if you want me to. I know it will be hard for you."

"Thanks. That would help. Dad can rant at you instead of me about what a jerk Brad is."

"I have broad shoulders."

"Hutch. I know we are supposed to love those who hurt us. Turn the other cheek and all, but right now, I hate Brad. I don't want him saved by the Blood. I want him to rot in the fires of Hell."

"Understandable, but not someplace you want to stay. Take it to the cross. Set your hurt, anger, betrayal, and hate there. Give it to the One who can heal it all. Then pray for Brad. You don't have to pray anything specific. Right now you probably can't. Just lift him, Kim, and the situation up. Ask for hearts to be changed; theirs and yours."

~~~~~

Turner ended the call. He ran his hand through his hair. This was the worst time he could have gotten it. He was on his way to Noelle's house. Hutch had texted that he was leaving, and he thought Noelle could use a little company. He was trusting Turner to help her get over her hurt, and not to hurt her more, now or in the future.

All he wanted was to be there for Noelle tonight, tomorrow, and forever. He could do tonight. Tomorrow, he was flying to Nicaragua. Of the future, he had no idea.

Plus he wouldn't get to see the boys before he left. They were with their father since it was Wednesday. He was surprised Brad took them for the night.

He frowned. Brad didn't deserve to have them. He didn't want them anyway. Turner did. He wanted their mother, too. Even more.

The desolation and defeat were palpable on Noelle when she opened the front door. Turner pulled her to him, then scooped her up into his arms and strode quickly into the great room. He settled them on the sofa with her on his lap. Noelle had wrapped her arms around his neck. She was crying.

"Ah, honey. Cry it out. I know it has to be devastating." Rather than pour ineffective words, Turner simply held her, stroking his hands up and down her back. It didn't matter how long it took her to release the emotions. He was going to stay right where he was, giving what comfort he could. When Noelle raised her head, Turner's heart ached at the desolation he saw in her eyes.

"How could he be so heartless? So selfish? How could I have married such a…" She paused searching for an adjective to describe Brad.

Turner placed his fingers on her lips. "Shhh. We both know what he is. You don't need to say it. It's not your fault. None of this. Sure, you may not be perfect, none of us are, but he made and is making his own choices. It's no reflection on you."

"How can it not be? I married him. Gave him two children."

"Two wonderful children whom he's thrown away. A special, beautiful, caring, loving woman. He definitely doesn't deserve you or them. I think it was a colossally stupid thing to do. But, you know, I'm glad he did. If he hadn't, I wouldn't be here with you now. I'd be sitting at Kyria's house, poorly decorated as it is, watching them make goo-goo eyes at each other."

Noelle giggled just a bit and laid her head on his chest. She sighed. "I do have to say I've been happier the last month than I had been in years. Brad was a great husband before Camden was born. After that, as I look back, he began to change. He didn't take much of an interest in the baby. He seemed annoyed that he took so much of my time and attention. Then after Mace was born, well, he began staying longer hours at work. He said it was so he could get ahead and provide for us better. Now, I think it was so he didn't have to be around us."

The comments struck Turner. Maybe that was more of the reason he and Kyria had been left in the care of Mamie and the various tutors. His parents were totally devoted to each other; neither one wanted to not be the focus of the other's attention. Their children would have been a distraction. Never would he do that to any child he was graced with, step or natural.

Turner laid his cheek against Noelle's head. He hated what he had to say next. All he wanted to do was stay here, holding her, giving her comfort. More than anything, he wanted to tell her of his love for her. And his love for Camden and Mace. That he wanted to marry her and be a father to her boys, and any more children they might have together.

But he couldn't. Things were too uncertain. After Morocco, Turner wasn't going to offer her a future when he didn't even know if he would live through the next couple of days. He'd not give her the happiness of those thoughts, only to have them snatched away in the blink of an eye. He might simply leave and vanish from the face of the earth. He wouldn't do that to her.

They sat in silence for a long time. Turner could tell she was relaxing, and he didn't want her to fall asleep in his lap. He shook her gently. "Noelle?"

"Hum?" She mumbled, snuggling a little closer.

"You can't fall asleep. As much as I'd like to stay here with you all night, you know I can't. I won't."

"I know." Noelle lay against him a few moments longer before she sat up. She looked at him, taking in his serious expression. Her focus sharpened, and her eyes fluttered back and forth as she studied his face. "You're leaving again. When? Can you tell me where?"

"I shouldn't say where, but I'm going to tell you. My flight leaves for Nicaragua at six tomorrow morning. If I don't come back, you'll know something to tell Kyria."

"Turner, no."

"Shhh, honey. Don't worry. It shouldn't take more

than a couple of days. I'll text you when I'm heading home. Don't expect anything until then." He gave a weak chuckle. "Maybe I'll even have you pick me up at the airport if the time's right."

"I would love to do that. I could even bring the boys."

"I would love that. I hate not being able to see them. To say good-bye."

He watched as her eyes filled once again.

"Ah, honey." Turner pulled Noelle close, and kissed her with every bit of the love he had for her but couldn't express. At least not yet. He just hoped he had the opportunity.

CHAPTER FIFTEEN

The driver opened the car door to let Turner get in. His flights had been delayed by a winter storm. He was a day late getting to the Central American country. He'd spent Thursday night in the Atlanta airport, hoping for it to break and allow his flight to leave.

On the seat was a black suitcase similar to the one he'd been supplied with in Morocco. Seems his message that he wanted to be armed carried on to this mission.

Turner had reviewed the detailed list of tasks he was supposed to complete before he returned to the States. Most were simple enough. Meet, assess, gather information using the contact lens camera and audio recording button. Those were normal, routine.

He knew there would be an additional piece of high tech equipment in the briefcase. With it, he'd be able to download all the data from a computer hard drive within seconds. All he needed was to be within ten feet of the device. It could hack computers, phones, or tablets. By the time he was finished collecting from every person he was to meet, he'd have terabytes of data.

At least he wouldn't have to wade through it. All he had to do was collect it and pass it off to his contact. No, all he had to do was live through it.

Once Turner was in his hotel room, he went through his normal routine of scanning for bugs and cameras. Finding none, he studied the items in the case. Everything was familiar, normal. Turner smiled at the comb with the ceramic knife in the handle. He'd liked that when he saw it in Morocco. Liked it so much he'd purchased his own. Of course, he'd had to leave it in the U.S. as it wouldn't make it through security.

Turner familiarized himself with the way the hacking equipment worked, and how it would avoid detection. Pretty simple, really. It looked like his hotel room key card. The logo was actually a fingerprint reader that would turn the device's hacking system on. Set with both Bluetooth and wireless capabilities, a slight depression within the plastic enabled him to activate the hacking by feel rather than sight. He didn't even have to take the card out of his pants pocket. The device would automatically begin pulling data from everything within range and continue until its memory was full. Once all data was pulled, it discontinued scanning automatically. Every byte would be encrypted. If the card was found, there was no way to figure out what it contained.

There were several hours before his meeting. Turner stripped down to his briefs and crawled into bed. He had time for a nap.

When he closed his eyes, all he could see was Noelle. The hurt she'd had the day before was so deep, so pervasive, he'd felt it radiate from her as soon as she'd opened the door. Oh, how he wanted to break every bone in Brad's body. Pull every hair from Kim's head. He grinned a little. He had the skills to do it, too.

But doing so wouldn't help Noelle. It would just be vengeance on the ones who had hurt the woman he loved.

He glanced at the briefcase and the items it held. Maybe some would say what he was doing was for the sake of vengeance. Turner wouldn't. God called for justice and mercy. What he was helping with would serve both. Hopefully, lives would be saved, and those who had taken so many would be stopped from continuing their murderous rampaging. And he, Kyria, and those they loved wouldn't be in danger any longer.

Looking up at the ceiling again, Turner prayed for God's protection on this mission and for the project to be completed and successful.

~~~~~

The alarm on Turner's phone woke him. He had an hour to get ready to be taken to the meeting. Rubbing the sleep from his eyes, Turner got up and went to take a shower. He studied his face in the mirror. Would this be the last time he brushed his teeth? The last time he looked at his reflection?

He shoved the morbid thought aside. He'd prayed. No matter how this turned out, he was secure in his God. Turner just hoped he wouldn't meet Him tonight.

Dressing carefully, he pocketed the key card hacker and concealed his weapons. The contacts were placed in his eyes, and the audio recording button tested. He'd just settled his sport coat on his shoulders when the room phone rang.

"Sí?"

"Your driver is here, Señor." The man's thickly

accented English was difficult to understand.

"Gracias. Dile que estaré abajo." Turner slipped the hacking key card into his pocket and left the room.

~~~~~

"Bienvenido, Señor Metcalf. Come in. The general is taking a call but will meet with you shortly." The man who greeted him was short and rail-thin. His hair was oiled back, which Turner thought matched his demeanor.

"May I offer a refreshment?" he said, when they arrived in the receiving room heavily decorated with gold leaf. "We will have dinner as soon as the General is available."

Turner wandered to the window and looked out. He put his hand in his pocket and pressed his thumb to the indent on the card. There was a desk nearby. If there was a laptop inside, he'd grab what he could from it. "Beautiful gardens, Señor."

The man walked up beside him. "My wife's passion."

"Will she be joining us for dinner?"

"No, she finds these business dealings tedious."

"Understandable."

"Forgive my delay." The loud, heavily accented voice caused both men to turn from the view. General Montor came forward, all smiles and outstretched hands. "Mr. Metcalf, finally we meet. I've heard a lot about you and your family. So very sorry for the loss of your parents. They were great friends of the people of Alawanda."

Turner nodded. "They loved the country very much."

"Yes, they donated much of what they earned from their businesses there."

"Are the schools and hospitals still functioning? The

upheaval in your country is often reported on our news. I never know how much is true or false."

"Sadly, much of it is true. The rebels have done much to destroy many of the advancements given from your parents, as well as others, to the people."

Turner merely nodded. That he knew was fake. The death and destruction was ordered by Emperor Demar Atul, the dictator who had taken over the country nine years ago. General Montor was his minion.

"Let us proceed into the dining room." Their host bowed them through the doorway.

Dinner was multi-coursed and delicious. Turner had to admit that. The general must not adhere to his religious convictions, as he drank several glasses of wine with the meal.

"Shall we adjourn to the señor's office, where we can continue our discussion without taking more of our host's time?" General Montor nodded, and smiled at the short man.

"Of course." Turner expressed his appreciation for the wonderful meal and hospitality he'd enjoyed, before he and the general moved to the office.

"I must again express my deep regret at the terrible accident that took the life of your parents. You must miss them very much." The general seated himself behind a massive wooden desk. It was dark with age and highly carved.

"Thank you."

"Now, let us get down to business. You've contacted my government to request consideration of the businesses confiscated during the rise to power of our glorious Emperor Atul."

"I am hoping we can come to some agreement about

recompense for revenue lost." Turner leaned back in his chair and slipped his hand in his pants pocket. Activating the device, he continued the false negotiation. He knew there was no way Atul would give up the equivalent of a dime to compensate the Metcalf family for their losses. The business loss mattered not. The value lost by the deaths of two people he loved could never be repaid.

Forty-five minutes later, their discussion had come to a close. The general would take the offer agreed to between he and Turner back to the small African nation. Both knew nothing would come from it. Turner doubted Atul would ever even see the report. Now, he just had to get out of the country alive.

Their host offered to have Turner taken back to his hotel, which was declined. Turner's driver was only a block away, waiting for him to call. Within five minutes, he was in the vehicle breathing a bit easier. So far everything had gone smoothly. He only hoped it would continue to do so.

"My flight leaves at nine tomorrow. Please pick me up at six-thirty."

"Sí, Señor. I will come to your room."

"Gracias. I will be ready."

~~~~~

Turner was up early. He hadn't slept well. Dreams of his parents, of their last time together, of the scene of the plane crash kept rousing him from slumber. Then pictures of the building Kyria worked in that he'd seen after the explosion. Noelle and the boys invaded his dreams too, waking him in a cold sweat. He couldn't wait to get on his plane and out of the country.

Packed and waiting, Turner paced the room. He

brewed some coffee in the small maker, took a small sip and grimaced. There was no way his stomach was going to handle the bitter brew.

A knock sounded on his door. Turner glanced at the clock by the bed. Six-twenty-five. He went to it, turned the knob, and knew immediately he'd made an elementary error.

Someone shoved hard against the door, knocking Turner, causing him to stumble back. A blade flashed. He tried to jerk out of the way. Piercing pain shot through his side. No, he wasn't going to be taken down this close to the end. The room door slammed, closing them in.

Turner let muscle memory take over. His left hand shot out and grabbed the arm that had stabbed him, forcing it up. His knee lifted and met groin. As the man bent, Turner's right hand jabbed into his throat. He felt the larynx crush. The man collapsed, struggling for breath. Turner, holding his side, blood dripping through his fingers, panted, trying to catch his.

A knock sounded. Turner looked through the peephole. It was his driver. He opened the door and stepped back, leaning against the wall.

The driver looked at the man lying on the ground. He swore in Spanish. "Señor, are you all right? No, we go to hospital."

"No, I need to get back to the States. I'm not safe here." The driver helped Turner over to the bed. "You tie him up. He'll need medical attention, but should be able to last until you get me to the airport. See if he has a phone. Check the messages, call history, and voicemail. If you can figure it out, text a thumbs up. That will hold them off for a while."

He took as deep a breath as he could. One handed, he opened his suitcase. He wouldn't be able to wear these clothes. The pants and shirt were covered with blood.

Pulling his phone out of his pocket, Turner activated an app. Once he'd stripped, he aimed the camera at his side, scanning it over the wound, around to the back then front several times. There was silence as the app processed. Then it dinged. "Medical attention required, but not urgent."

Turner got a T-shirt out and, with the driver's help, put it on. He pressed another app on the phone and the shirt shrank, pressing tightly against his sides. "That will stop the bleeding until I can get home."

"It will?"

"I hope. It's supposed to. Help me get dressed."

As soon as he was clothed and his suitcase repacked, they left. After dropping Turner at the airport, the driver would come back and deal with the assailant. Turner didn't care what happened to the man and wouldn't ask. That was up to the driver and his commanders.

It seemed as if he'd walked a million miles when he finally got to the gate. Fortunately, the line at security hadn't been long, and the compression shirt didn't set off the scanner when he went through. Now, all he had to do was get on this plane, make his connection, and he'd be back in Benton.

Thankfully, he was a first-class passenger and so boarded first. The flight attendant took one look at him and asked if he was okay.

"I'll be fine. Had a slight accident on the way to the airport. I just need some time and quiet." He'd bought some pain medication in a shop as he went to his gate. Once he was settled, he cracked open the water bottle and swallowed the tablets.

The flight was smooth, and he'd slept some. The pain in his side receded as he sat still. Turner dreaded the walk through the long corridors to customs and immigration. Every airport seemed to compete to have the longest distance between arrival gates and the entrance into the domestic airport terminal. Turner thought Atlanta was the winner.

Several times, he stopped and leaned against the wall to catch his breath. He praised God that he'd decided to check his bag rather than carry it on. He didn't think he could have pulled it the entire way.

"Sir, are you all right?" A uniformed customs agent placed a hand on his shoulder.

For a brief moment, Turner thought to say, yes he was fine, but decided to be at least partially honest. "I'm having some difficulty with this walk. I injured myself early this morning. I just need to get home so I can have it looked at."

"Let me get you a courtesy cart." The agent called, and, within five minutes, Turner was seated and being driven to immigration, then on to his gate. He tipped the driver a hundred dollars.

There were only a few minutes to wait before boarding began. Noelle would be home, or at least able to answer her phone since it was Saturday. The boys should be with Brad. He actually hoped they would be. Turner wanted her to pick him up. He desperately needed to see her. Maybe she could even tend to his wound.

He dialed, praying she would answer.

"Turner? Are you back?" The relief in her voice nearly broke him.

"I'm in Atlanta. Will be boarding in a few minutes. Can you pick me up?"

"Of course. Turner, is something wrong? You don't sound too good."

"I'll tell you about it when I get to Benton." He bit back the 'I love you' he wanted to say. The first time he told her, Turner wanted her in his arms.

Just as he finished giving her the flight information, the boarding call was announced. Turner struggled to rise, but was gratified that as he stood and walked, he seemed to get a little stronger.

Settling into his seat, Turner prayed the flight would be smooth. It wasn't. Though he tried to relax, each bump and jostle made his muscles tense and pain shoot through his side.

As soon as they landed and turned onto the taxi strip, Turner activated his phone. It beeped several times, indicating multiple text messages.

Missed you in Atlanta.

Complications?

Meet in Benton airport?

Turner typed his reply. *Yes, yes, no. House.*

Then, he texted Noelle. *Landed. Please meet me at baggage claim.*

He breathed a sigh of relief when she responded with a thumbs up.

Waiting until everyone else was off the plane, Turner made his slow walk along the jet bridge. Benton airport wasn't large, but it seemed so as he traversed the concourse toward baggage claim.

CHAPTER SIXTEEN

Noelle watched as the crowd of people flooded into the baggage claim area. She'd expected Turner to be one of the first. She knew he flew first-class, so would be one of the first off the plane. Once the initial passengers surged around the still carrousel, she moved to the corridor they had come through.

As she continued on toward the security exit, Noelle began to get worried. Turner hadn't sounded himself when they'd spoken.

When she first saw him walking slowly toward her, Noelle was relieved. Then, concern and fear took over. He was pale and sweating, walking with his hand touching the wall as he watched every plodding step his feet were taking. Something was wrong. She picked up her pace to just short of a run.

"Turner?"

He lifted his head and looked at her. "Hi, honey, I'm home."

"What's wrong? Are you ill? You look terrible." Noelle barely managed to keep her hands from fluttering around him, searching for what was the matter.

"We can talk in the car. Let's get my bag and get out of here."

He began his careful walk again. Noelle slipped herself under his arm wanting to support him. The sharp intake of his breath made her realize he'd been injured.

"Do you need a wheelchair?" she murmured, shifting to his other side.

"No, you being here is what I need."

Wanting to move quickly, but knowing he couldn't, warred within Noelle. Most of the people and baggage were gone by the time they reached baggage claim.

"Tell me which bag is yours and I'll get it. You shouldn't try to lift it." Noelle stopped beside a pillar and made Turner lean against it. Once she had the suitcase, she came back and inserted herself under his arm again. "I'm going to leave you by the door and go get the car. You don't need to walk to where I'm parked."

"Sounds like a plan. Thanks."

There were seats in front of the floor to ceiling windows near the doors, so she left him there, taking the suitcase with her. Noelle nearly ran to the car. Should she take him straight to the hospital? That's what she wanted to do, but didn't think he'd agree.

Pulling out her phone, she called Mark. "Turner's been injured. I'm at the airport. Just met him. I'm getting the car now. Are you home?"

"Yes, but…"

"I know he won't go to the hospital. At least, not until you tell him he has to go. I'll bring him straight there."

"Should I get Keith?"

"I don't know. All I know is that he's injured on the left side. He's pale and sweating. He's walking, but leaning pretty heavily on me."

"Okay. I'll call Keith. We may both have to convince him to go if needed."

"Thanks, Mark. We'll be there as soon as we can."

"Just drive safely."

"I will."

Noelle threw the suitcase in the back of the SUV, and took out a couple of blankets. Turner was only wearing a sport coat. If he'd lost a lot of blood, he'd chill easily.

As soon as she pulled up to the curb, putting the car in park, she unbuckled and threw open the door. Turner was making his way out the double doors. He was even paler than before, if that was possible.

Noelle opened the passenger door and helped him in. She covered him with the blankets, and hurried around to get in.

"I called Mark. He's at home. He's calling Keith. I don't know what happened, but it's going to get fixed as soon as possible."

She glanced at Turner. His head was leaned back against the headrest. His eyes were closed.

"I want to take you straight to the hospital."

"No." Turner looked at her. "Not if Mark and his buddy can fix this."

"What happened?"

"Stabbed. I crushed the other guy's larynx though, so I'm better."

She chuckled. "Typical man."

~~~~~

Mark and Keith came running out of the house when Noelle pulled into the driveway. By the time she turned the car off, they had Turner between them, practically carrying him as they hurried up the walk. Kyria stood to the side, wide-eyed with her hands pressed against her mouth. Noelle ran to her. They hugged, and followed the men as they took Turner to his room.

"What happened?" Kyria asked. She and Noelle stood in the doorway watching as Mark and Keith began cutting Turner's clothing off.

"What's this?" Mark asked. The button-down shirt was gone, revealing the compression shirt. He draped a sheet across Turner's legs and hips.

"Pressure shirt. Stabbed. Stopped the bleeding," Turner said. "Give me my phone."

Noelle ran forward and picked up the remains of his slacks. She fished the phone from the pocket, handing it to him. He swiped and pressed, and the shirt began loosening. Blood began seeping. Not a lot, but it stained the fabric and caused Kyria to gasp.

"Noelle, take Kyria and wait out in the living room," Mark said.

"But I can help."

"Kyria needs you now," Keith spoke for the first time.

Noelle glanced at him and saw the determination in his eyes. She looked at Mark, then Kyria. The young woman was white, looking as if she might collapse. She hurried over. "Come. We will just get in the way here." Taking Kyria by the hand, they left the room. Noelle pulled the door closed behind them.

"What happened?" Kyria asked, turning terrified eyes toward Noelle.

"I don't know. You know he went to Nicaragua, didn't you?"

"Yes."

"Do you know why he's been traveling so often?" Noelle asked.

"He just says it's a business trip. Some project."

"That's what he's been telling me too. He's hoping it is completed soon. He's hinted that it's dangerous. I get the idea he's known something could happen to him."

"And now he comes home stabbed in the side."

Kyria fell back to sit on the sofa. Noelle joined her. They huddled together, wrapping their arms around each other and pulling close, sharing what comfort they could.

Noelle hadn't a clue as to how much time had past when Turner's door opened, and Mark came out. She and Kyria jumped up, running to him.

"He's going to be very sore for a while, but he'll recover. He was extremely fortunate. Not a single major organ or artery was damaged. He said the last flight was rough and pulled quite a lot. That's probably why he was bleeding some when the pressure shirt was released. We cleaned the wound and stitched it up."

"Can we see him?" Kyria took the words out of Noelle's mouth.

"Shortly. Keith's helping him into some sleep pants and a shirt. We knew you'd want to know the extent of his injuries." Kyria pressed herself against her husband, weeping her relief.

Noelle felt tears slip down her cheeks. She didn't have anyone to hold her. The one she wanted to was lying in a bed in the other room.

"Come here and get a hug," Mark said. "You look like you need one." He held out his arm, inviting her to join them. Noelle accepted the invitation.

~~~~~

Turner lay back against the pillows. Keith might be a very good surgeon, but he left much to be desired in helping someone into clothing. Stitched and bandaged and sore and tired, Turner was surprisingly hungry. Arching over all that, he wanted Noelle beside him. Needed her.

"You have some explaining to do to a couple of women out there," Keith said. "I'm curious too. It's not often I get called to fix a stab wound in the brother-in-law of my best friend."

Turner knew he shouldn't tell any of it, but at the moment he didn't care. His cover was blown. He'd suspected it in Morocco, and Nicaragua confirmed it. No way was he going on another mission. Hopefully, whatever information the hacking device had gathered would be enough.

Turner took a deep breath and jerked in pain. "Go get Noelle and Kyria. They'll want to see I'm alive and kicking. Maybe not kicking much now, but I will be soon. Then see if I can get something to eat."

Keith saluted and left the room. Seconds later, Kyria, followed closely by Noelle, flew in. One went to the left, the other the right, and both kneeled beside the bed.

"Are you all right?" The words were spoken simultaneously.

Turner reached a hand to each of the women he loved more than life itself. "I will be soon. Right now, I hurt pretty badly. That husband of yours isn't a light-handed doctor. He prodded and pulled until I thought he was going to tear me apart."

"If you'd gone to the hospital, like you should have,

they'd have given you something to either numb it or put you out." Kyria's voice didn't hold much sympathy.

Noelle giggled. "She's right. Your own fault."

"Come sit with me. I won't break." Turner patted the bed on both sides of him. Noelle was on his uninjured right side, so he pulled her close.

Keith came in carrying two straight chairs. Mark followed with two mugs. "Soup and coffee." He held up one, then the other.

Turner was glad they allowed him a few sips of each before the questions began. What happened? What's going on with all these trips that are obviously not business trips? What are you involved in? Are you in danger here? Are we in danger and why?

Turner finished the soup and gave the mug to Kyria, who set it on the bedside table. "You all deserve an explanation. It's not an easy thing to explain."

"Whatever this is, it's why you hired security protection for us all, isn't it?" Noelle asked.

"What?" Kyria and Mark gasped.

Turner looked at each person. He'd hoped that little detail could be left out, but Noelle's question nixed that. "Yes, there's been twenty-four/seven protective details over you both." He indicated Kyria and Mark. "Noelle and the boys, and your entire family, Mark, for several weeks. I wasn't going to take any chances that anyone would be threatened or harmed." He looked at Keith. "I may hire coverage for you and your fiancé now, too. At least until things are complete."

"What things?" Kyria asked. "What's going on?"

Turner looked at her, trying to decide how much to reveal. He knew her, despite what she thought. Even though he'd been pretty much absent from her life for so many years, he'd kept in touch with Mamie as well as her bodyguards. Uncle Russ had kept him filled in too. What he was going to tell her would settle undeserved guilt upon her shoulders. Nothing she'd done had caused the events that led them to this day, but his sister would take up that burden.

"You know of Demar Atul of Alawanda?"

"That horrible dictator who keeps killing his people?" Kyria asked.

"Yes, you knew Metcalf Industries and Development had several concerns in Alawanda. Beside the mining and agricultural ventures, Mom and Dad were building hospitals, schools, supporting small industries by locals. That was all before Atul came to power. They were instrumental in the advances the country was experiencing. Then, Atul took over. He confiscated all the businesses. He killed the local representatives and kicked the foreigners out of the country. Metcalf Industries protested. That was just before the crash." He didn't need to explain what crash. Kyria knew.

Her hand flew to her mouth. "Oh no. It wasn't an accident."

Turner shook his head. "No, it wasn't." Noelle, who was holding his hand, gave it a gentle squeeze. "They didn't care about the money involved. If Atul had left the hospitals and schools, they wouldn't have cared. Well, they wouldn't have liked losing so much, but that wasn't their main concern. They wanted the people of Alawanda to have the benefits they were beginning to receive from all Metcalf had done for them.

"I was traveling pretty heavily at the time. I didn't want to be involved in the business. Blamed Mom and Dad's interest in it, rather than you and me, for just about everything. I liked being able to do what I wanted with the money the businesses supplied, but didn't want to help make it.

"Then Uncle Russ contacted me. Told me about the crash. Even then, he thought something didn't seem right about it. Their pilot was experienced. He'd been with them for years. You remember him. He used to give you candy whenever you were on the jet. Me too, when I was younger."

Kyria nodded. Tears were slowly slipping down her cheeks. Mark came and sat beside her on the bed, putting his arm around her.

"About a year after, I was contacted by the government. They had information that Atul was going after any foreigners who had business connections in the country. They were concerned there might be more 'accidents.' Several other people had died.

"There was also a group of Alawandans who were looking for help to overthrow Atul. They were needing not only money and arms but information."

Kyria gasped. "You're a spy."

Turner glanced at Noelle, who had sat up and was looking at him, nodding. "You figured that out?" He asked her.

"Yes, after your last trip. All the secrecy, how you phrased things while trying to explain."

"When I was first asked, I was hesitant. I didn't want to get involved. Then, they told me about another business owner whose son was killed in a suspicious accident. That's when I decided to help.

"Most of the time when Uncle Russ and you didn't know where I was — I was training or on light missions, learning and being tested."

Turner stopped. This was the part he was dreading most. He took as deep a breath as his injury would allow and slowly let it out. "That bombing of the building you worked in? It was meant for you, Kyria."

"What?" She nearly screamed the word.

"You were supposed to die in the explosion. Atul is trying to take out anyone who might have a claim to a business in Alawanda."

"But you don't want the business, do you?" Kyria's shock and horror came through in her tone.

"No, I told the authorities that when they first contacted me. They told me it didn't matter. That Atul was going to eliminate anyone who might be able to influence or financially support any opposition to his rule. You've heard what he does to his own people. It's been all over the news."

The doorbell rang, and Keith went to answer it. Silence filled the bedroom as each person absorbed what Turner had been saying.

"What about Ben's family, and that of the others who were killed in the explosion?" Kyria asked. "I set up college funds for all the children, and gave each family a settlement. Now, finding out it was because of me…"

"Those have all been augmented. They all think it's from the government. A terrorist compensation."

"Good. To think that it's my fault…"

"No, Kyria, it's not your fault. The responsibility is all on Atul. He's caused it, not you. You're as much of an innocent bystander as any of the others who've been hurt or killed. That's what I'm helping to stop."

Keith came back in, followed by a man in a black suit.

"Howard, thanks for meeting here. I know it's out of

protocol. Not too sure I could have met you anywhere else today."

"Understandable."

"This is my contact, Howard Mitchell." Turner went on making the introductions.

"I remember you," Mark said. "You came to the hospital and questioned Kyria after she woke from her coma."

"Yes." He didn't elaborate. "Were you successful?"

"Depends on what you are referring to. I'm alive, does that count as a success?" Sarcasm laced the words. Turner noted just a slight flush of the spy contact's cheeks. "As to the other, you'll have to determine that from the card. I hope it will have all you need. I'm done. My cover's blown, and with the injury, I won't be fit to go for a while anyway."

Turner had Noelle get the card from the pile of items from his pants pocket, that were on the bedside table near her. Keith had emptied his pockets before taking the ruined clothes from the room. She gave it to the agent.

"I'll give you a couple of days to file your report. Glad you weren't injured more." He turned and left the room. Keith followed to see him out.

Turner closed his eyes. The pain meds he'd been given were beginning to take effect. There was no way he could stifle the yawn.

"Okay, everyone out. The patient needs to rest," Mark stood and helped Kyria off the bed.

"Stay a minute, Noelle, please," Turner said.

"Okay."

Once they were alone, Turner put his hand behind her neck and brought her to him, kissing her with an intensity he'd never allowed himself before. Their previous kisses had been passionate, but into this one he poured all his longing, desire and love.

"I love you, Noelle. I couldn't tell you before. I wanted to, but knew the danger I was involved in. Revealing my love and then possibly dying, maybe leaving, and just vanishing wouldn't be fair to you. I just thank God that He allowed me to come back to you."

Tears slipped down Noelle's cheeks. "I love you too. I was so afraid you were just having a fun time over the holidays with me and the boys. All those silly mice." She gave a weak grin.

"I think I fell in love with you when you were standing on that picnic table, telling me there was a mouse this big." He stretched his arms out. The movement pulled on his side. "Ouch."

Noelle giggled. "You be a good patient." She leaned over and kissed him. "If you're awake before I leave, you'll get another one of those."

"Now, I won't sleep at all."

"Sleep. That's an order from your personal nurse."

"One more kiss, please." Turner made begging puppy-dog eyes at her.

She laughed and leaned down, lightly brushing his lips with hers. "Sleep."

"Yes, ma'am."

CHAPTER SEVENTEEN

Christmas morning was going to pose a problem for Turner. He was torn between opening gifts with Kyria and Mark and wanting to be with Noelle, Camden, and Mace. The latter would be the most fun, but he hadn't spent Christmas with his sister in years. Mark solved the problem for him. They'd all go to the Christmas Eve service, complete with its play, then he, Kyria, and Turner would open their gifts that night. Noelle was planning on putting the boys to bed as soon as they got home, since the following day would be exciting and filled with activity. Turner wanted to hug him for the idea, but fist bumped instead.

He was still sore, but was healing. Mark had him on a course of powerful antibiotics to ward off any infections. Camden and Mace had been warned that, until further notice, there would be no wrestling or rough-housing. Mace forgot once when Turner arrived and jumped at him, wanting a hug. No harm done, but he did get scolded by his mother.

Now, they were sitting in church with the play beginning. Camden sat on one side of him, Noelle on the other with Mace on her lap. Turner glanced over

Camden's head at Kyria. She turned her head and smiled at him.

Even though he didn't have a house in Benton, Turner was home. He didn't think he'd ever felt that in any other place. Sure there were some houses owned by him and Kyria. Places they'd spent some time as they grew up, but none held any special memories. They were all just one of the many locations they had traveled during those years.

Here, in Benton, was home. Kyria was here. It's where any of her children would be born. Mark was becoming like a brother. They'd gotten to know one another while he was living with them. Turner respected him, and the way he treated Kyria had turned that into love for the man.

Mark's family had welcomed him with open arms. He was attending the Jenner family Christmas dinner tomorrow. Turner had received a call from Mark's dad, Will, inviting him in a way that left him positive he was wanted. That Noelle and the boys would be there as well tipped the scales from feeling like an obligated invitation to knowing he was wanted. There was little reason for the Jenners to invite them. They were relatives of Hutch, but that didn't necessarily mean they would be included.

It would be a noisy gathering. Mark had two brothers as well as his sister, Chloe, Hutch's wife. Each one was married with children. Turner couldn't wait. He'd never been to a large family gathering for Christmas. He was adding to the noise by bringing gifts for all the children, party noise makers that shot out into filled paper tubes with a feather on the end when blown. The adults might hate him for it, but he'd make points with the kids.

The lights dimmed and worship service began. Turner took Noelle's hand, holding it while they listened to the familiar words of Luke, and how Jesus came so we could be reconciled to the Father.

~~~~~

Noelle spooned scrambled eggs onto two plates, and set them in front of her sons. They were excited for Turner to arrive, and the presents that were finally going to be opened.

When the doorbell rang, both boys jumped from their chairs and ran down the hall. Noelle could hear noisy greetings of "Merry Christmas." She put bacon strips onto a platter that already had sausage links waiting to be eaten.

"Hello, Sweetheart. Merry Christmas." Turner kissed her on the cheek as he placed a bag on the counter. As the boys climbed back onto the high stools, he took two jars out. "Raspberry preserves and lemon curd. Yummy on crumpets." He pulled a bag of the English bread out and held it high.

"You don't eat trumpets," Mace said. "You blow them."

Noelle laughed. "Crumpets, silly, not trumpets."

As they ate, Turner told of the tradition of crumpets for Christmas.

"We didn't have a lot of traditions and that bothered Mamie. She said everyone needed some special thing you only did on Christmas morning to help mark it as special. So, she started one for Kyria and me. It was the only day of the year she made crumpets. Also, we never had raspberry jam and lemon curd together any other time of the year.

"The crumpets were freshly made that morning. As each of us got old enough, we were allowed to help make them. They're pretty easy, but can flop pretty badly when made by an eight-year-old. I bought these yesterday at the bakery, so they aren't quite as good, but fine in a pinch."

"I think they're great," Mace said, red jam and yellow curd smeared across his cheeks.

"Me too." Camden took another big bite of his. It broke in two, and one piece tumbled down his pajamas.

Noelle let Turner clean up the kitchen while she got the boys dressed. She thought she heard the front door open and close, and wondered what he was up to. When they went into the great room, Turner stood in front of the Christmas tree with a huge smile on his face. Behind him were three presents much larger than the others. They were three different sizes. Noelle looked at him with suspicion. She hadn't agreed to additional gifts.

"What's this?" She asked. The boys were examining the extra large gift bags. Each one found their name on a huge tag.

"Can we open these now, Mommy?" Camden was bouncing, and Mace was ready to tear the ribbon off as soon as she gave permission.

"There's one for you too, Noelle." Turner said, stepping aside to reveal her name on the tag of the largest present.

Noelle opened her mouth to speak.

"No, don't say anything until you open yours. I know we didn't talk about this, but it'll be okay." Turner gave her a quick kiss. "Go ahead, guys. Open them up."

Noelle decided now wasn't the time to start arguing

that he shouldn't have purchased more gifts. Besides, one was for her. The shapes in the gift bags had clued her in on what might be inside.

"A bike. My own bike," Camden yelled. "Thanks, Turner."

"Mine's green. I love it. Thank you." Mace came and gave him a hug.

"Mine's blue."

The bikes matched, although Mace's was smaller. Both had training wheels. Helmets were tied to the seats. Camden was busy undoing the ribbon so he could climb on.

"Open yours," Turner whispered into Noelle's ear.

She pulled the bow, and he helped her get the red folding cycle out of the bag. Even though she'd only seen his folding bike once, Noelle knew this was a slightly smaller model. She also knew it was an expensive bike.

"Turner." He kissed her to stop her protest.

"I got these so we would be able to ride this spring and summer. Theirs aren't expensive bikes. Just ones they can crash and enjoy. Yours is similar to mine. We can take some rides, just the two of us. I've already cleared it with Hutch and Chloe, that they'll watch the boys when we want to go."

Noelle's throat clogged. If he was planning on riding with them during the spring and summer, that meant he was staying in Benton.

"Thank you," she managed to choke out.

"You're welcome." Turner hugged her to him and kissed her. "I love you."

"I love you too."

"Enough with the mushy stuff. Let's open presents."

Mace pushed between them.

~~~~~

Later in the morning, they all piled into the Macan, with the usual argument over its color. Everyone had been delighted with their gifts. There were now many more small plastic bricks scattered over the floor. They'd migrate into the playroom later, but for now, they'd been enjoyed in the great room.

Turner had helped Noelle make the salads she was bringing to the Jenners'. When he cut himself chopping cucumbers, she'd kissed his finger and put a bandage on it. That had led to more kisses, until the boys started making gagging sounds.

Turner glanced at Noelle. She was fingering the heart pendant he'd given her. It was an open, stylized design with small diamonds in one of the curves. She'd protested that it was too expensive. He'd countered that he'd purchased it at a department store.

They were greeted warmly by the Jenners. As soon as everyone arrived, they would open the small gifts they gave each other. Turner had the noisemakers for the children and gift certificates to a local coffee shop for the adults. He hadn't had to bring any gifts, but wanted to thank them all for their hospitality in including him in their celebration.

There was also one more gift for Noelle. He'd dropped it off the day before, explaining what and why to Mark's parents. It was tucked behind the tree, and would be the last gift handed out.

As everyone was gathering in the living room, Kyria came to stand next to Turner. "Lovely necklace you gave Noelle. I'm surprised she allowed you to give her something so expensive. How did you convince her?"

"I just told her it came from a department store. That satisfied her."

"Oh? Which one?"

"Neiman Marcus."

Kyria laughed. "Just the most expensive department store in the country."

"Hey, she didn't ask which one."

"Come, let's all sit down and begin as we always do," Will Jenner said. As soon as everyone was mostly quiet, he picked up a worn Bible. "This Bible was my great-grandfather's. It's really old," he told the children gathered around. "We only read from it on Christmas morning. Even though it's old, the words are the same." He opened the book and began reading about the birth of Christ from the Gospel of Luke.

~~~~~

As Turner had known, the noisemakers were a favorite gift of the children, and he got hate filled stares from their parents. He didn't care. Mark's brothers, sister, and spouses were laughing as the children tried to blow the paper tubes into each other's faces. The toys wouldn't last long, and most would be left at the grandparents' house when the day was over. Then they'd just disappear.

"Hey, there's one more present back here," one of the children said. Turner hadn't a clue which child it was or whom she belonged to. He bit his cheek to keep from smiling too much and giving away any clue as to who had brought it.

"It's for Aunt Noelle," one of the older boys said. He looked to be about eight.

"Me?" Noelle was sitting next to him on a love seat.

"Yeah, it doesn't say who it's from." The boy brought

the gift over, handing it to her. Everyone stopped what they were doing to watch her open it.

Noelle shook the box. It was about the size a pair of tall boots would come in. Her name was printed on a computer label stuck on the front.

"Open it," one of the younger Jenner girls said, coming close to watch.

Noelle tore the paper off. When she lifted the lid, she smacked Turner on the arm. "You," she laughed. Flipping the box over, out fell a myriad of white, gray, and black furry little stuffed mice. The same ones he and the boys had been hiding.

The children fell upon them, laughing and tossing mice up in the air and at each other.

"How many did you get?" Noelle asked.

"A gross."

"How much is a gross?" Camden asked, tossing a mouse at Noelle.

"One hundred forty-four." Turner tossed it back at him.

"Wow, that's like a million."

All the adults laughed.

~~~~~

After they had eaten, the younger children were put down for naps. The others were playing quietly with toys they'd received that morning and brought with them. Most of the women were in the living room chatting, and the men were in the theater room watching football. Turner had been sent on a popcorn run and was in the kitchen when Mark came running in.

"Come on. You have to see this. We paused the TV. We need to get Kyria, too."

All the adults gathered in front of the large screen. Will pressed the button and the news anchor began.

"We interrupt this program to announce that Demar Atul, self-proclaimed emperor of Alawanda, has been ousted in a coup by the rebel forces, along with much of the military. Although unconfirmed, the rebels are claiming Atul, and his highest military leader, General Tagan Montor, have been killed in the rebellion.

"Atul took power nearly nine years ago. Until that time, Alawanda had been one of the rising stars of the African continent. They were advanced in their schools and hospitals, as well as social programs to help the population escape poverty. Since Atul's rise to power, the country has been filled with genocide, and the destruction of much of the infrastructure, along with most schools and hospitals."

Turner sat down heavily. They'd done it. They'd successfully taken their country back from a homicidal maniac. He looked at Kyria. She was white. Her hands clasped over her mouth. Mark wrapped his arms around her. She accepted his embrace, tucking her head under his chin.

"This is great news, but what does this have to do with you?" Hutch asked.

Noelle slipped onto the chair Turner was sitting on, and put her arm around his waist. He couldn't speak. His throat seemed paralyzed.

"There's evidence that Atul was instrumental in the plane crash that killed Kyria and Turner's parents. Companies they owned had interests in Alawanda. They built a number of the schools and hospitals that man destroyed," she explained.

Everyone sat in silence. The football game went on

with the sound muted. Several hands patted Turner on the back showing sympathy. He could barely think. It was over. The fear that he or Kyria, or someone they loved, would be murdered just to satisfy the greed of an evil man, had simply ended.

Turner didn't know how he felt. He'd never really expected the threat to ever be over. Never thought the rebels would be successful. But they had been.

"Look," someone said.

Across the bottom of the screen ran a ticker. *Confirmation has been received that Emperor Atul and General Montor have been killed in the presidential palace in the capital of Alawanda. Watch the News at 9:00.*

That broke Turner's paralysis. He swept Noelle into a tight hug and kissed her silly. He jumped up and grabbed Kyria. "It's over. God handed out His justice." Turner shuddered. He looked at Kyria, Mark, then Noelle. "General Montor was who I met with on that last trip."

"Oh, Turner." Noelle came over. He let go of Kyria and pulled her into his arms. He kissed the top of her head.

"It's over. It's finally over." Now, Turner thought. Now I can start to actually plan for a future.

CHAPTER EIGHTEEN

Noelle hated that she was born three days after Christmas. It was bad enough to have a name that screamed the holiday, but her birthday had always been overshadowed by the birthday of the Savior. Her parents had tried to convince her that it was an honor to be born so close to Christmas. That hadn't ever worked. Her siblings had birthdays ranging from late April to September. They all got presents both for Christmas and their birthdays. Their days were made special with cake and ice cream. By the time her birthday came, everyone was sick of leftovers and Christmas cookies.

Turner had said he was going to make hers special this year. He had a plan. Hutch, Chloe, and Noah, as well as Mark and Kyria, were coming to her house for a party. Turner had kicked her out of her own house, telling her to go get a facial or massage, or some other girly thing. He and the boys were cleaning and setting it all up. She figured there would be mouse decorations all over the place when she got back.

Noelle hoped he'd get over the mouse teasing soon. It was getting a little old. The boys still enjoyed it. She'd had to scream again that morning when she found a mouse in her underwear drawer. Seems they had a new supply of the toys since Christmas. Oh well, it was fun for them and didn't do any harm.

Sitting in a coffee shop, sipping from the expensive latte she'd spent her gift certificate on, Noelle thought over the last couple of months. Was it really less than two since she had met Turner? It seemed as if she'd known him forever. Trying to figure out when she had fallen in love with him, she realized it had just crept in, sort of like how a mouse sneaks into your house. You didn't notice at first, then the evidence of its presence becomes more and more apparent.

Turner was much better than a mouse. He was funny, affectionate, played with the boys, and he cleaned up after himself. That was a definite plus. And he was staying in Benton after the New Year. Another plus.

They'd sat next to each other last night, after the boys were in bed, looking at real estate sites online. Not having to consider the price of a home was something foreign to Noelle. She was surprised that he didn't seem interested in the huge homes that she'd surmised someone of his wealth would want. When asked, he'd said they were too big. Too easy to keep away from the rest of the family. He'd grown up being both not seen and not heard. That wasn't something he wanted his home to be.

Noelle was also surprised that he was asking her opinion. Sure, he'd said he loved her, but hadn't done or said anything to make her think she was going to play a big part in his life other than how they were now.

That thought depressed her further. She did come with baggage after all. That's the way many men looked at women with children. As much as Turner liked her boys, it was different to want to take on the responsibility of raising them.

Well, she was working herself up into a pretty dismal funk. Deciding she needed to quit the pity party, Noelle swallowed the last of her latte, pasted a smile on her face, and went to the nail salon next door that took walk-in clients.

~~~~~

Turner was finding out what having two very excited boys was all about. He'd brought in all the decorating supplies for the party as soon as Noelle left. That Camden and Mace were disappointed with the theme he'd chosen was very apparent. They complained about the colors, the paper plates, the cups, the tablecloth. Just about everything until he sat them down and explained his idea.

"This isn't your party. What did you have for your party Camden?"

"Superheroes."

"What about you, Mace?"

"Paw Patrol."

"So, each of you had a party with something you really like."

They nodded.

"So, what should Mommy's party be?"

"Something she likes?"

"Right." Turner fist bumped each boy. "So, all this stuff is what girls like."

Camden's face lit up. "I get it. We show Mommy how much we love her by giving her a party of stuff she likes."

"Right. Are you ready to help me get this place decorated for her?"

"Yeah," both boys shouted.

When the decorating was complete, Camden asked, "What about the food? Are we going to have to eat junk like what Kim likes?" Mace wrinkled his nose and stuck out his tongue.

"Nope. Uncle Hutch and Aunt Chloe are picking up from Bonacelli's Italian Garden. That sound good to you?"

"Yeah, I love their s'getti. Did you order that?" Mace asked.

"Just for you, squirt." Turner tapped him on the nose. He looked at his watch. "Okay, guys. Let's get you changed into your party clothes. Everyone will be here shortly."

By the time he'd managed to get the boys dressed, everyone but Noelle had arrived. Turner poured himself a glass of the wine Mark had brought. He needed it. He was exhausted.

"I don't know how Noelle does it. She works full time, runs the house, and does everything for the boys. I've only had them for an afternoon, and I'm wiped out."

Mark laughed and patted him on the shoulder. "She's used to it and so are they. You're new and special and exciting. Makes them harder to handle."

"You did great, big brother," Kyria said. "The decorations are perfect. She's going to love it. No red or green except on the tree."

"We didn't take that down. The boys protested. Said they always left it up until New Year's. I figured it wouldn't spoil the ambiance."

"Compromise. A glorious word. Works with children and women," Hutch said.

"Men too, sweetheart," Chloe said. She picked Noah up, and took the finger foot Noelle had received for Christmas, out of his mouth.

They heard the garage door opening, signaling Noelle's arrival. Everyone gathered in the kitchen to greet her as she came in.

"Happy Birthday!" was shouted, Camden and Mace rushing forward to hug their mother.

"We decorated just for you," Camden said.

"We's having s'getti from Bon's garden. Uncle Hutch brought it." Mace bounced around the kitchen.

Turner stayed back while the others greeted her. When they stepped back, he brought her to him, encircling her with his arms. "Happy birthday. Many happy returns." The kiss he placed on her lips was long but gentle. "Yummy, you taste like chocolate." He licked his lips.

Noelle laughed as she stepped away and began taking off her coat. "I treated myself to one of those really decadent chocolate, pecan turtles. I ate the whole thing myself."

"Good for you," Kyria said.

Chloe agreed. "Great treat for your special day."

Noelle hadn't noticed the decorations yet, so the boys pulled her into the great room.

"Look, Mommy. You're the princess."

Turner watched as she took in the pink and purple streamers. The gold and white balloons hanging from the light fixtures. The tablecloth had every Disney princess ever created, he thought. Princess plates were waiting for cake. Princess cups were filled with ice and water.

"You did this all for me?" Noelle looked at Camden and Mace, then at Turner after they nodded, smiles a mile wide on their faces.

"It's to show how much we love you. Even if superheroes would have been better," Camden said.

Turner ruffled his hair. "Hey, who's this party for?"

"Can't Mommy be a superhero?"

"She is, but she's a princess too."

"Come open your presents." Mace pulled her to the sofa. There were presents on the coffee table. Not one was wrapped in Christmas paper.

When she opened the mouse watering can with the artificial flowers, Noelle laughed. "I knew there would be some mouse for my birthday. At least I can't kill this plant."

She threw the mouse socks that read 'warm my toes' Turner had given her at him.

Everyone else laughed at the tattoo sleeves. The boys were excited about them since they had bought them at the cycle shop. "They go with your new bike," Camden said.

They ate and cut the princess cake. Then, with Noah asleep on Hutch's shoulder, he and Chloe headed home. Mark and Kyria weren't far behind, taking time to clean up the rest of the dishes.

Noelle took the boys to get them ready for bed. Turner paced. He had one more gift. One that would change his life forever.

"Come tell the boys goodnight." Noelle stood in the hall and held her hand out for him.

Turner took it and brought it to his lips. "At last we'll

have a few minutes of quiet."

Noelle laughed, and pulled him down the hall to the boys' room.

Once prayers were said and hugs and kisses deposited on sleepy foreheads, Noelle turned off the light and closed the door. Turner stood waiting for her in the hallway. He smiled, and put his arm around her shoulders as they went to the great room.

"Well, princess, did you like your party?"

"It was wonderful. I may have had a themed birthday when I was little, but normally, it was just a cake nobody wanted to eat and whatever presents weren't combined with a Christmas gift. Thank you."

"I aim to please."

They sat close together on the sofa, Noelle tucked against his side, his arms around her. It felt so right, so — Turner could only think of one word. It was home. Being with Noelle and the boys was home. It didn't really matter where they were. They were home to him.

"Noelle, I have one more present for you." Turner took a small box out from under a pillow where he'd placed it earlier. He slipped to kneel on the floor. "I love you. I love the boys. You're everything to me. I've known for a while, even though we haven't been acquainted very long, that you were my future. I couldn't do or say anything until the situation with Atul was completed. I didn't know if I had a future to offer you. Now, I do.

"Noelle, will you marry me?" He flipped open the box, revealing a brilliant cut diamond ring. Small diamonds were set all around the band.

Her hand was shaking when she reached out and touched his cheek. "Oh, Turner. This has been the best, most wonderful birthday I've had in a long time. You came into my life and transformed it. Took me from just handling everything, to enjoying it again. I love you. Of course, I'll marry you."

Turner slipped onto the sofa and took Noelle into his arms. He looked deep in her eyes. In them, he saw love, home, and his future. He smiled and lowered his mouth to meet hers.

A long time later, they sat quietly, simply enjoying each other's presence. She sat with her back to his chest. His arms were around her while she admired the ring on her finger.

"You know," Turner said. "There was this giant mouse at the toy store. I thought about getting it for you, maybe tying the ring around his neck."

"I'm glad you didn't. All the mice have been fun, funny. The boys have loved teasing me with them. But this, the way you proposed. It was perfect."

Turner dropped a kiss on her head. "It would have been fitting though. A giant mouse brought us together. Helped us meet. A giant mouse could have brought us to marriage."

Noelle chuckled. "Mice and marriage. Who would have thought they'd go together?"

CHAPTER NINETEEN

EPILOGUE

Turner heard the office door close, but didn't swivel the executive chair around. Instead he waited. He'd been trained to be patient. Let the man, who'd been called to his boss's office, sweat. However, the 'boss' was taking a few minutes making rounds of the lower executives. Instead, Turner was sitting at his desk.

A throat cleared.

Turner waited a couple more minutes. Let the man sweat. It placed Turner in an even more powerful position than he already occupied. With a slight push with his foot, he rotated the chair. His elbows rested on the arms. His hands clasped loosely in his lap.

"Mr. Copeland, I wish I could say it was a pleasure seeing you."

"You? What are you doing here?" Brad Copeland

jerked straighter as he stood in front of the desk.

"I have a proposition for you. One that benefits both of us."

"What can you offer me that I'd want?" Brad sneered.

"Several things actually. Let's count them off. Continued employment within the company. Covering the cost for your move to the California office. Relieving the burden you carry supporting two young boys for, oh let's see, fourteen more years of child support."

"Just how are you going to do that?"

Turner leaned forward and pushed a folder across the desk. "Simple, you read and sign those documents giving up all parental rights to Camden and Mace. That will end your commitment to them, and allow me to adopt them once Noelle and I marry."

"Why would I ever do that? They're my sons." Brad picked up the folder and removed the papers.

Turner nodded. "Biologically, yes. In actuality, not so much. I overheard you telling the bimbo you're living with about your wedding and career plans. Noelle knows about it, too.

"Now, you can sign those papers releasing the boys or, well, it would be a shame if the transfer fell through, and you were suddenly out of a job."

"Who do you think you are, threatening that you'll get me fired?"

"Oh, did you not know? I own this company as well as its subsidiaries. I believe you are an employee at will. If you don't understand the term, it means I can fire you at my will for any reason at all. Will you sign, or do I call security to have them escort you from the building. My building."

"That's blackmail."

"It's called protecting my family. A family you don't want and threw away. I heard you and the bimbo talking about how you were going to the Bahamas for a destination wedding. That you were moving to California with your job transfer. That you were looking forward to not having the boys very often. That they were a nuisance.

"You have big plans for your future. How long would Bimbo Barbie, like, hang around if you were unemployed? If you, like, couldn't take her to the Caribbean for, like, the wedding or move to California?"

Brad flipped through the papers he held. "What's this?" He threw several sheets of paper onto the desk. Turner picked them up and studied them for a moment.

"Oh, can't you read them? They are a listing of all the dates you didn't take the boys for their scheduled time with you. Judges like documentation. Noelle has every time for nearly the past year listed here. As you can see," Turner slid the papers toward Brad again, "The dates get closer and closer as they progress. In the past couple of months, you declined to have them more times than you had them. Wonder what a judge would think of you forfeiting your Thanksgiving with them."

Brad just looked at him. He focused on the documents again.

Turner waited in silence and set a pen on the desk.

Brad pinned Turner with a stare. He laid the papers on the desk and picked up the pen.

"Wait," Turner said. He pressed a button on the phone. "Ms. Donovan. Will you please come in and bring your notary stamp?"

Moments later a knock, and the door opened.

"Please witness Mr. Copeland signing these documents."

Once everything was finished and they were alone again, Turner stood. He moved around the desk to stand in front of Brad. "I think you've made the correct decision for both you and Noelle, Camden, and Mace. Thank you. To show you my sincere appreciation, I'll upgrade your flights to the Caribbean to first-class. As I stated before, I'll also pay for the expenses you'll incur with your move to California."

Brad's expression brightened. Turner was disgusted with the man's avarice. He was surprised and dismayed that Brad hadn't protested the relinquishing of his parental rights more forcefully. It revealed the man's self-centered character.

"Please feel free to come and explain to the boys that you will be leaving their lives when you move."

Brad cleared his throat. "I'll come to say goodbye, but you and Noelle can tell them you are going to be adopting them."

Turner nodded. He'd figured Brad wouldn't want to tell his sons he was abandoning them to be raised by another man.

~~~~~

Turner was pleased but uncertain. Having Brad give up parental rights to Camden and Mace might have been easy to accomplish, but telling Noelle, that might be a bit more difficult. Her telling the boys would be hard too.

Yesterday, Turner had spent a couple of hours with Hutch. They'd talked over Turner's idea about Brad.

Although he knew it was the right thing for the boys and Noelle, Turner didn't want to cross the line. Skirt it maybe, just enough to get Brad to sign the papers.

Both men knew how the news that Brad had given up his sons would affect Noelle; she'd be devastated for the boys. Hutch had suggested he and Chloe invite Camden and Mace to stay overnight with them. That was always a treat. Noah was old enough to enjoy them being there. That way Turner could tell Noelle without the boys being around. They could discuss, and Noelle could cry. Then they'd plan on how to tell Camden and Mace.

When Turner pulled into her driveway, the garage door was open. Her car was inside. She never left the door up. He did a quick check of his jacket pockets. The documents were in a large inside pocket on the back.

Turner went to the back door and tried the knob. The door was locked. He hoped that was a good sign. He knocked. Noelle opened it a few moments later.

"Hey. Come on in." She kissed him then backed out of the way. "I'm making adult food for supper; shrimp stir-fry."

"What's with the garage door being open?"

She shot him an annoyed look. "The boys stuck one of those mice on the safety eye. Knocked it out of alignment. Now, it won't close. You wouldn't know how to fix it, would you?"

"Um. Maybe? I can try. Never have before." Turner lifted his shoulders doubtfully.

Noelle put her hands on her hips. "You know the rule: You make the mess. You clean it up. That goes for fixing your little mice prank mess up, too."

Turner went out and took out his cell phone. He had an app that shot a laser beam. Getting down on the floor, he held the phone against the electric eye, pointing the laser across the doorway. It took only a few moments to shift the eye into alignment, and for the garage door to start to go down.

Turner went back into the kitchen. "Success."

"How'd you do it so quickly?" Noelle was adding the shrimp to the wok.

"I just used a mousecatool." Turner waved his phone in the air. "My laser app."

"For aligning garage door electric eyes?"

"A laser to help see how off center it was." Turner went to the sink and washed his hands.

"You've been watching too many Mickey Mouse Clubhouse episodes with my boys."

Turner grinned at her and moved to one of the bar stools at the counter, slipping his jacket off and hanging it on the back. He was glad they were going to eat now. It put off the subject he needed to bring up. *Some spy,* he thought. *You're a chicken when it comes to your woman.* Well, he wasn't a spy anymore.

They chatted as they ate. Noelle must have suspected something was amiss. She kept shooting inquiring glances at him.

As soon as she wiped the counter after they'd filled the dishwasher, she said, "Is something wrong? Oh no, you have to travel again, don't you? I thought that was all over."

The near panic in her voice made Turner reach for her and pull her against his chest. "No, honey. No travel in the foreseeable future. At least not without you and the boys. Come and let's sit down. There is something I want to discuss with you." As they moved toward the sofa, Turner grabbed his jacket off the bar stool.

"You going somewhere?" Noelle asked, flipping a hand at his jacket.

"I have something in a pocket I need to get out."

"Just how many pockets does that thing have? And how heavy is it with all that you have in them."

"You know, I've never counted. It's fairly heavy." Turner made pumping iron motions. "Keeps me strong."

"Doofus," Noelle said as she flopped down on the sofa.

Turner knew the smile she had on her face could very well change to tears in a few moments. How did one take the ultimate rejection of the father of their children?

He took the papers out and laid them face-down on the coffee table, and sat down beside her.

"I went to see Brad at his job today."

Noelle drew her eyebrows together in confusion. "Why? How did you get in? They keep that place pretty secure. I had trouble getting in when I needed to."

"It helps when you own the company."

"You own T&K Accounting Consultants?"

"Well, Kyria and I do. Our parents set it up a couple of years after Kyria was born. It was in a trust until Kyria turned twenty-one. T&K, Turner and Kyria."

Noelle's jaw dropped. "They have offices all over the country. They're one of the leading accounting firms."

"All over the world actually."

Turner waited for more questions, but she was just

looking at him. He decided the topic of his business holdings and net worth, etc. could wait for another time.

"I went to T&K to speak with Brad." He picked up the documents and handed them to her.

Noelle began reading. He watched as the color drained from her face. She looked at him. "What did you do?"

"I could say that I wanted to see how dedicated Brad was to being a father. While that was revealed, it wasn't my main reason for doing this. Hutch and I talked this over at length yesterday. With Brad making the move to California, now was a good time to make the break permanent. If Brad wanted to keep his rights, I'd know this attitude was temporary. That he was a man who might come to his senses and truly be a father to Camden and Mace.

"I did put some pressure on him. I'll admit, I would have fired him if he hadn't signed. What he's done to the boys shows a lack of character that's not appealing to a business owner.

"I also showed him copies of the notebook you have recording, all the times he missed having the boys. It added a bit of incentive.

"The entire conversation took no more than twenty minutes." Turner didn't add that he'd gotten a call from the head of the Benton branch, saying Brad was boasting how he knew the owner and had been specifically chosen for the California office. He was even having his moving expenses paid for by the company. Turner had called the manager of the California branch Brad was transferring to. He'd told him to put Brad on notice that any infraction would lead to his termination with cause.

"Why? Why would you want to take my boys' father from them? As poor a one as he is, Brad still is that."

"Noelle." Turner took the papers she was crumpling in her fist and laid them on the table. "Camden and Mace deserve a father who loves them and will be active in their lives. A father who will put them before everyone but their mother. I want to be that person. Brad doesn't. Not only did he give up their mother, he gave up being their father for nothing more than a bit more money and a bimbo.

"Getting Brad to give up his rights and responsibilities did a couple of things. It confirmed what you already knew. He doesn't want them to be part of his life. It also made it possible for me to adopt them."

Noelle's mouth dropped open. "You... You..."

"Yes, once we're married, I want to start adoption proceedings. I love them nearly as much as I do you. I want them to be my sons. Not just my stepsons. My sons. If you'll let me, that is."

The tears he had been afraid would appear did. They slipped over her eyelids and down her cheeks. It broke his heart. How would he ever repair the damage he'd done?

Noelle leaned over and kissed him, hard. "No one has ever done something so wonderful for me. I was so concerned Brad would want them next summer, then ignore them the entire time. That he'd not contact them, and then would, and then not.

"But you— you wanting to make Camden and Mace yours. That's the most wonderful gift you could ever give to me."

"I promise, I'll be the best father I can possibly be to them. And the best husband to you. We'll make sure they don't hate Brad when we explain to them. I want them to feel as secure and loved by you and me as we can."

Turner wrapped his arms around her and sealed his promise with a kiss. Or was it kisses? Definitely kisses. Several hours of kisses until he got up to leave.

Reaching for his jacket, Turner jumped a bit, startled. Noelle started laughing. He began to laugh too. He picked up the little black mouse sitting half-hidden under the collar of his jacket.

"Seems we've had a witness to our discussion."

"Discussion— is that what they are calling it these days?"

"I refuse to call it making out."

Noelle stood and took the mouse from him. "You know what? I think we should have a mice-themed wedding reception. These little guys brought us together. They should be witnesses to our marriage."

Turner pulled her in for another kiss. "That sounds like a great idea."

A NOTE FROM SOPHIE

I hope you enjoyed **Mice and Marriage**. Please take a moment to leave a review on Amazon. For independently publishing authors like myself, the reviews are extremely valuable in getting our work noticed. <u>If you take just a few minutes you could help someone else find their next favorite book.</u>

You can post a review right from your Kindle or Kindle app. Just scroll past the end of the book. The form will pop up. Although Amazon says they require 20 words they will post it with fewer. You can pad your review with the title of the book and author name.

Find more of my books on Amazon: http://amazon.com/author/sophiedawson

To keep up with my sales and upcoming releases, sign up for my newsletter: https://mailchi.mp/449be73f3465/sophiedawsonnewsletter

Join my Sophie's Reader Friends group on Facebook.

Thank you.

Sophie